D0643477

The Climates of Love

MODERN ROMANCE CLASSICS
General Editor Michael Levien

This series presents outstanding twentieth-century novels by British and foreign writers whose central themes are love and romance. Other titles are in preparation.

PUBLISHED

MICHAEL SADLEIR These Foolish Things
ANDRÉ MAUROIS The Climates of Love

André Maurois

The Climates of Love

Translated from the French by
VIOLET SCHIFF AND ESMÉ COOK

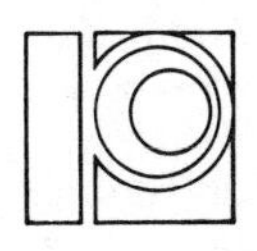

PETER OWEN · LONDON

ISBN 0 7206 0671 3

Translated from the French *Climats*

PETER OWEN PUBLISHERS
73 Kenway Road London SW5 0RE

First published as *Climats* 1928

This edition published 1986 by arrangement with the Estate of André Maurois

Printed in Great Britain by
A. Wheaton & Co. Ltd, Exeter

À SIMONE

Toujours nous voulons chercher l'éternel ailleurs qu'ici; toujours nous tournons le regard de l'esprit vers autre chose que la présente situation et la présente apparence; ou bien nous attendons de mourir comme si tout instant n'était pas mourir et revivre. A chaque instant une vie neuve nous est offerte. Aujourd'hui, maintenant, tout de suite, c'est notre seule prise.

ALAIN

PART ONE

ODILE

ODILE

I

My sudden departure must have surprised you. I apologise but do not regret it. I wonder if you also hear the storm of music which has arisen within me during the last few days, like the highest flights in Tristan? How I wish I could abandon myself to the passionate impulse that only the day before yesterday urged me towards you in your white dress in the forest; but I am afraid of love, Isabelle, and of myself. I do not know what Renée and others may have told you of my life. We have sometimes talked about it: but I did not tell you the truth. The charm of making new friends lies in the hope of presenting one's past to them in a favourable aspect. Our friendship is no longer at the stage of flattering confidences. Men deliver up their souls as women their bodies by successive well defended zones. One by one I have thrown my most secret forces into the fray. My true memories, hitherto concealed, will reveal themselves and appear in the light of day.

Here I am, far from you, living in the room where I spent my childhood. There is a shelf on the wall full of books which my mother has kept for more than twenty years, 'for my eldest grandson', she says. Shall I ever have sons? The large red-backed ink-stained book is my old Greek dictionary, those with gilt bindings are my prizes. I want to tell you everything, Isabelle, from the time I was a sensitive child, then a cynical adolescent, until I was a wounded unhappy man. I want to tell you all, simply, accurately and with humility. Perhaps if I finish writing this story I shall not have the courage to show it to you. Never mind. Even if I write this account of my life for myself only, it will not have been in vain.

You remember one evening, coming back from St. Germain, I described Gandumas to you. It is a sombre, beautiful region. A torrent flows between our factories, constructed in the heart of a rather wild gorge. Our house, a small sixteenth century château like so many to be seen in Limousin, dominates a heather covered moor. At an early age I was proud of being a Marcenat and happy that our family ruled over this district. From the small paper works that had served as a laboratory for my maternal grandfather, my father had made a vast factory. He had bought back the leasehold fields and transformed Gandumas, which before his time had been almost waste land, into a model property. During my childhood I watched the construction of buildings, and saw the big shed for pulping paper gradually extending along the banks of the stream. My mother's family belonged to Limousin. My great-grandfather, a lawyer, had bought Gandumas when it was sold as national property at the time of the French Revolution. My father, an engineer from Lorraine, had only lived in this part of the country since his marriage. He had brought one of his brothers here, my Uncle Peter, who lived at Chardeuil, the neighbouring village.

On Sundays, when it was fine, our two families met at the Saint-Yrieix ponds. We drove there in our carriage. I was seated opposite my parents on a hard narrow folding seat. The monotonous trot of the horse made me sleepy; I amused myself by watching its changing, distorted shadow on the village walls and banks as we passed by, and resuming its normal shape when we turned the corners. From time to time a smell of dung, which like the sound of bells was linked in my mind with the idea of Sunday, enveloped me like a cloud; large flies settled on me. I disliked the hills most of all; the horse walked and the carriage ascended at a tediously slow pace while the old coachman Thomasson clicked his tongue and cracked his whip.

At the inn we found my Uncle Peter, his wife and my cousin Renée, their only daughter. My mother gave us bread and butter and my father said 'go and play'. Renée and I walked about under the trees or at the edge of the ponds and gathered pine cones and chestnuts. When we returned Renée came with us and the coachman managed to make room for her on the edge of the folding seat. During the journey my parents did not speak. Conversation was always made difficult by my father's excessive reserve. He showed concern whenever any intimate reference was made in public. When we were at table, if my mother said a word about our education, the factory, our uncles, or about Aunt Cora who lived in Paris, my father indicated by an embarrassed gesture that the servant was changing the plates. My mother then stopped talking. When I was very young I noticed that if my father and my uncle had any fault to find with one another they always got their wives to convey it with special precautions. I also saw that my father had a horror of frankness. With us all conventional sentiments were true, all parents always loved their children, all children their parents, and all husbands their wives. The Marcenats wished to see the world as an earthly paradise and it seems to me now that their attitude was more ingenuous than hypocritical.

II

The sunlit lawn at Gandumas. In the plain below, the village of Chardeuil was veiled by a haze of shimmering heat. A little boy, up to his waist in a hole he has dug near a heap of sand, watches the wide landscape for an invisible enemy. This game was inspired by reading my favourite book *La guerre de Forteresse* by Danrit. In my sharpshooter's hole I was Private Mitour and was defending the fortress of Liouville, commanded by an old colonel for whom I would gladly have laid down my life. Forgive me for mentioning such childish sentiments but in them I find the first expression of my need for passionate devotion which has been one of the dominant factors of my character, although it has since been applied to very different objects.

If I analyse the imperceptible particles of memory which still remain to me of the child I was then, I recognise a touch of sensuality in my desire for self-sacrifice.

However my play very soon took a new form. Another book, a New Year's gift entitled *Little Russian Soldiers*, was about a group of schoolboys who decided to form an army and chose a student called Ania Sokoloff for their queen. 'She was a remarkably beautiful, slender, elegant and skilful girl' – I liked the oath taken by the soldiers to the queen, the labours they accomplished to please her and the smile that was their reward. My ideal woman, whom I have so often described to you, came partly from that story.

I see myself walking beside her on the lawns at Gandumas; she talks of sad and beautiful things in a low voice. The pleasure she gave me was always mingled with the idea of daring and risk and I called her the Amazon.

I also enjoyed reading with my mother the stories of Lancelot of the Lake and Don Quixote. I could not believe that Dulcinea was ugly and had torn the drawing of her out of my book so as to imagine her myself.

Although I was two years older than my cousin Renée we did lessons together for a long time. When I was thirteen my father sent me to the lycée Gay-Lussac at Limoges where I stayed with one of our cousins and only came home on Sundays. I had inherited my father's taste for study and reading, liked school life very much, and was a good pupil. The pride and timidity of the Marcenats were growing in me as inevitably as their bright eyes and slightly raised eyebrows. The only antidote to my pride was the queen to whose image I remained faithful. I had now given her the name of Helen, because of my admiration for the Helen of Homer, and my professor in the second form, M Bailly, was responsible for this adventure. Why do certain pictures remain as clear for us as when we first saw them, while others, seemingly more important, are hazy and quickly effaced? At this moment I see M Bailly wonderfully vividly in my mind's eye entering the classroom with his slow step. He hung his shepherd's cloak on a peg and said 'I have found a fine subject for your French composition "The Recantation of Stesichore" . . .'

I can still see M Bailly clearly. He has a thick moustache, close cropped hair and a face strongly marked by passions, no doubt unhappy ones. He takes a paper from his portfolio and dictates: 'The poet Stesichore, having cursed Helen in his verses for the evils she brought down upon the Greeks, is stricken with blindness by Venus and then, understanding his guilt, composes a recantation in which he expresses his regret for having blasphemed against beauty.'

How I would like to re-read today the eight pages I wrote that morning. Never again have I found that perfect fusion of inner life with the written word, never, except perhaps in a few letters to Odile and, hardly a week ago, in a letter destined for you which I did not send. The theme of self-sacrifice to beauty awoke in me such a deep responsive chord that in spite of my extreme youth I felt afraid and worked for two hours with almost painful ardour, as if I had foreseen how much reason I too would have during the course of my difficult life on earth to write the recantation of Stesichore.

But I should be giving you a false idea of the soul of a schoolboy of fifteen if I did not tell you that my state of exaltation remained entirely hidden within me. My conversations with my schoolmates about women and love were cynical. Some of my friends spoke of their experiences with technical and brutal details. Helen was embodied for me in a young woman from Limoges, Denise Aubry, a friend of the cousins with whom I lived. She was pretty and was considered rather fast. When anyone said in my presence that she had lovers I thought of Don Quixote and Lancelot and should have liked to attack the slanderers with a lance. The days Mme Aubry came to dinner I was mad with joy and fear. Everything I said when she was there seemed to me absurd. I detested her husband who was an inoffensive and kindly manufacturer of china. I always hoped to meet her in the street when returning from school and having noticed that she often went at midday to buy flowers and cakes in the rue Porte-Tourny opposite the cathedral, I contrived to be on the pavement between the florist and the pastry-cook at that hour. Several times she allowed me to accompany her to her door, with my school-satchel under my arm.

When summer came I saw her more easily at the tennis

courts. One evening, as it was fine, several young couples decided to dine there, and Mme Aubry, knowing quite well I was in love with her, asked me to stay too. Supper was gay and night began to fall: I was lying on the grass at Denise's feet when I touched her ankle and my hand gently enfolded it; she made no objection. I can still smell the strong scent of the syringas behind us. Stars could be seen through the branches. It was a moment of perfect happiness. When it was completely dark I heard rather than saw a young man of twenty-seven, a lawyer of Limoges well-known for his wit, creeping towards Denise, and, without intending to, I overheard their whispered conversation. He asked her to meet him in Paris at an address he gave; she murmured, 'be quiet', but I understood she would go. I still held her ankle and she, happy and indifferent, took no notice. But I felt wounded and suddenly conceived a savage contempt for women.

At this moment I have on my table the schoolboy's diary in which I made notes of my reading. I see in it: 'June 26. D', an initial surrounded by a small circle. Underneath I had copied a sentence from Barrès: 'We must take little heed of women, enjoy looking at them and pride ourselves on the pleasure we can derive from such unworthy objects.'

During that summer I ran after girls. I learned that one could take them round the waist, kiss them and play the fool with them in dark alleys. The episode of Denise Aubry seemed to have cured me of being romantic. I had devised for myself a routine of courtship which succeeded with a certainty that filled me with pride and despair.

III

The following year my father, who for some time had been a county councillor, was made senator for Haute-Vienne. Our way of life changed. Gandumas now became only a summer residence for us. I completed my course of philosophy at a college in Paris, and was to read for a degree in law and do my military service before choosing a career.

In the holidays I saw Mme Aubry again when she came to Gandumas with my Limoges cousins; I had an idea that it was she who had suggested coming with them. I offered to show her the park and took great pleasure in leading her towards a summer-house that I called my observatory where I had spent whole Sundays in a vague reverie at the time I was in love with her. She admired the deep wooded gorge in which one could see the foam breaking over the stones and the smoke rising from the factory. When she stood up and leaned forwards to see the distant movements of the workmen better, I put my hand on her shoulder. She smiled. I tried to kiss her; she gently pushed me away. I told her I should be returning to Paris in October, had taken a little flat on the left bank and hoped to see her there.

'I don't know,' she murmured, 'it is difficult.'

In my diary for the winter of 1906-7 I find many appointments with D. I was disappointed in Denise Aubry. I was wrong. She was a nice woman, but I had foolishly expected her to be interested in my studies as well as being my mistress.

She came to Paris to see me and also to try on dresses and hats. For this I despised her. I lived in books and could not understand others being different to myself. She asked me to lend her Gide, Barrès and Claudel about whom I talked to her so much; what she said to me about them afterwards annoyed me. She had a lovely body; I wanted her badly as soon as she returned to Limoges. When I had spent two hours with her I wished to die, disappear or have a talk with a man friend.

My two favourite friends were André Halff, an intelligent but easily offended young Jew whom I had met at the Faculty of Law, and Bertrand de Jussac from Limoges who had entered Saint-Cyr and came to spend his Sundays with us in Paris. When I was with Halff or Bertrand I seemed to enter a world of deeper sincerity. On the surface was the Philippe of my parents, a simple creature, made up of a few Marcenat conventions, then came the Philippe of Denise Aubry, subject to moods of tenderness and sensuality followed by violent reactions; the Philippe of Bertrand, courageous and sentimental; that of Halff, precise and hard, and I knew well that underneath there was still another Philippe, more real than all the rest. He alone could have made me happy if I could have been in harmony with him, but I did not even attempt to know him.

Have I told you about the room I rented in a little Pavilion in the rue de Varenne and which was furnished in the austere taste I had adopted at that period? Masks of Pascal and Beethoven hung on the bare walls, strange witnesses of my amorous adventures. The divan that served me as a bed was covered with coarse grey canvas. On the mantelpiece were Spinoza, Montaigne and some books on science. Was this done to impress or from a sincere love of ideas? Perhaps it was a mixture of both. I was studious and inhuman. Denise often told me that my room frightened her, but she liked it all the same. She had already had several lovers and always dominated them. She attached herself to me.

I mention this with humility. Life teaches us that modesty is easy where love is concerned. The least attractive can succeed, the most seductive fail. If I tell you that Denise cared for me more than I cared for her I shall tell you with the same sincerity of far more important episodes in my life where the situation was just the reverse. During the period of which I am speaking, from the age of twenty to twenty-three, I was loved but did not love. In truth I had no notion what love is. The idea that it could make one suffer seemed to me absurdly romantic. Poor Denise, I can see her now, lying on the divan leaning towards me and trying desperately to read my mind, which was completely closed to her.

'Love' – I said – 'what is love?'

'You don't know what it is? You will know – you too will be caught.'

I noticed the word 'caught', which I thought vulgar. I disliked Denise's vocabulary. I was annoyed with her for not speaking like Juliet or Clelia Conti. Her mind provoked in me the kind of response one feels at the sight of a badly cut garment. I pulled backwards, then forwards, in search of an unattainable equilibrium. I learned later that in Limoges she had earned a reputation for intelligence and my efforts had procured for her a lover who was one of the most difficult men to please in that part of the country. The minds of women are thus composed of the successive deposits brought to them by men who have loved them, just as the tastes of men preserve the confused, superimposed images of the women who have passed through their lives, and often the acute suffering a woman has made us endure becomes the cause of the love we inspire in another and, in turn, of her unhappiness.

M was Mary Graham, a young English girl with veiled mysterious eyes whom I had met at my Aunt Cora's. Aunt Cora was a sister of my mother. She had married a banker, Baron Choin, and had always been ambitious to attract to her house the largest possible number of ministers, ambassadors and generals. She had formed her first circle through being the mistress of a well-known politician. She deserved success for exploiting this advantage with admirable skill and perseverance.

She was at home Avenue Marceau every evening from six o'clock and on Tuesdays gave a dinner party for twenty-four people. Her dinners were one of the few subjects our Limousin family made fun of. My father maintained that she had never interrupted the series. In the summer they were transferred to the villa at Trouville. My mother told us that when my uncle was dying of cancer of the stomach, she had come to Paris to help her sister, and on her arrival one Tuesday evening she found Cora arranging the table.

'How is Adrian?' she asked.

'He is very well,' Aunt Cora replied – 'as well as his condition permits: only he won't be able to dine at table.'

The next morning at seven o'clock a servant had telephoned to my mother: 'The Baroness regrets to inform Mme Marcenat that the Baron died suddenly during the night.'

At the time of my arrival in Paris I had no wish to see my aunt, as I was brought up by my father to have a horror of society, but when we got to know each other I rather liked her. She was very kind, glad to be of service to others, and through her contact with so many men of varied activities had a real if slightly confused knowledge of the workings of society. Being a young provincial with an enquiring mind, I found her a ready source of information. Seeing that I enjoyed listening to her she made friends with me and I was invited to the Avenue Marceau every Tuesday evening. Perhaps there was an added touch of coquetry in her welcome on account of my parents' hostility to her salon and she was not averse to triumphing over them by annexing me. Naturally Aunt Cora's circle included a certain number of girls, a necessary bait. I decided to make love to several of them, although I did not care for them, if only to prove to myself that such conquests were possible for me. I remember how calmly I sat down in an armchair and took up a book, the moment one of them, smiling tenderly, had left my room and how easily I put her image out of my mind.

Do not judge me severely. I believe that many young men like me, if they do not have the good fortune to find a mistress or a remarkable wife early in life, inevitably behave with arrogant selfishness. They are looking for a philosophy of life. The women instinctively know that such a quest is fruitless and follow them half-heartedly. At first, desire creates an illusion, then between two almost hostile spirits an incurable boredom sets in. Did I still think of Helen of Sparta? Very seldom, but from time to time I discovered what was left of that sentiment in the depths of my soul, as in clear weather one might discern a submerged town under the sea.

Sometimes at the concerts I went to on Sundays I caught sight of an enchanting profile in the distance which reminded me with a strange shock of the fair Russian queen of my childhood and the chestnut trees of Gandumas. Then during the rest of the concert I offered to this unknown person the intense emotions roused by the music, and for several moments it seemed to me that if I could know this woman I should find in her the perfect almost divine being for whom I desired to live. Then the deposed queen was lost in the crowd and I rejoined a mistress I did not love in the rue de Varenne.

Today I find it difficult to understand how I could shelter two such contradictory personalities at the same time. They lived on different planes and never met. The tender lover, eager to offer devotion, had realised that the beloved woman did not exist in real life. Refusing to confound a vague beautiful image with a vulgar counterfeit he took refuge in books and loved no one but Mme de Mortsauf and Mme de Rênal. The cynic dined at Aunt Cora's and made bold and suggestive remarks to his neighbour, if she attracted him.

After my military service my father offered me a partnership in his factory. He had now moved his offices to Paris where his clients, the big newspapers and publishers, were accessible. His business interested me very much and I developed it while continuing my studies and reading. During the winter I went to Gandumas once a month; in the summer my parents lived there and I spent several weeks with them. I was glad to resume the solitary walks of my childhood in Limousin. When I was not at the factory I worked, either in my room which was unchanged or in my little observatory above the ravine of the Loue; every hour I got up and went to the end of the long avenue of chestnut trees, and returned at the same rapid pace to my reading.

I was relieved to be rid of the young women in Paris who had woven around my life a web of appointments, grievances and gossip, difficult to evade. Mary Graham about whom I spoke before, was the wife of a man I knew well; I disliked shaking hands with him. Most of my friends, on the contrary, would have done so with pride. But the tradition of my family in such matters was strict. My father had made a marriage of convenience, which became as often happens a love marriage. He was happy in his silent and reserved way and never had any amorous adventures, at least not since his marriage; yet I divined in him something romantic and confusedly imagined that if I had the good fortune to find a woman who resembled my Amazon a little I could, like him, be happy and faithful.

IV

During the winter of 1909 I had two attacks of bronchitis in succession and towards the end of February was advised by my doctor to go to the south for some weeks. I preferred to visit Italy where I had never been and after seeing the northern lakes and Venice, I decided to stay for the last week of my holiday in Florence.

The first evening in my hotel at the table next to mine, I noticed a girl of such rare beauty that I could not take my eyes off her. She was accompanied by her mother, still young, and an elderly man. Later I asked the headwaiter who were my neighbours. He told me they were French, Mme and Mlle Malet, and that their companion, who was not staying at our hotel, was an Italian general. At lunch time the next day the table was empty.

I had letters of introduction and presented one to Professor Angelo Guardi, the art critic, whose publisher was one of my clients; I received an invitation to tea from him the same day. In the garden of his villa in Fiesole I found about twenty people, among them were my two neighbours. The girl, wearing a large straw hat and a holland dress with a navy blue collar, appeared to me as beautiful as the evening before. I suddenly felt shy and moved away from the group in which she was standing to speak to Guardi. In front of us was a pergola covered with roses.

'I made the garden myself,' said Guardi, 'ten years ago all this ground you see was a field. Over there . . .'

In following his gesture I met the eyes of Mlle Malet and saw with surprise and pleasure that they were fixed on mine. It was the briefest of glances but held within it the minute seed, charged with unknown forces, from which my greatest love was born. I knew without a word that I could be natural with her and approached her as soon as possible.

'What a lovely garden!' I said.

'Yes, what I love about Florence is that one sees mountains and trees everywhere. I hate towns that are only towns.'

'Guardi told me that the view from behind the house is very beautiful.'

'Let's go and see,' she said gaily.

There was a thick curtain of cypresses divided by a flight of stone steps leading up to a rocky niche that sheltered a statue. Further off, to the left, was a terrace looking over the town. Mlle Malet rested her elbows on the wall near me and gazed for a long time in silence at the pink domes, the large gently sloping roofs of Florence and the blue mountains in the distance.

'Oh! how I love this,' she said, with a girlish graceful movement, throwing back her head as if to breathe in the landscape.

Odile Malet treated me with confiding familiarity, and told me her father was an architect, whom she admired very much. He had remained in Paris and it distressed her to see the Italian general dancing attendance on her mother. After ten minutes we were exchanging the most intimate confidences.

I talked to her about my Amazon and how impossible it was for me to find any happiness in life unless I could be inspired by a deep and passionate sentiment. (My cynical theories had been instantly swept away by her presence.)

She told me that one day, when she was thirteen, her best friend, Misa, said to her: 'Would you throw yourself over the balcony if I asked you to?' And she had been on the point of jumping from the fourth floor. The story enchanted me.

I asked her whether she enjoyed visiting churches and museums.

'Yes,' she said, 'but what I like best is to wander about in the old streets . . . I have a horror of going out with my mother and her general, so I get up very early in the morning. Would you like to come with me tomorrow morning? I shall be in the hall of the hotel at nine o'clock.'

'Yes, indeed I would . . . Ought I to ask your mother's permission to take you out?'

'No, leave that to me,' she said.

The next day I met her at the foot of the stairs and we went out together.

The large flagstones of the quays glistened in the sunshine, somewhere a bell tolled, carriages passed quickly by. Life suddenly became very simple. It would be happiness to have her fair head always near me, to hold her arm crossing a road, and feel for a moment the warmth of her young body under her dress.

We went to the via Tornabuoni; she liked the shops where they sold shoes, flowers and books. On the Ponte Vecchio she stopped for a long time looking at the artificial jewellery, necklaces of heavy black and pink stones.

'Don't you think it is amusing?' she said.

Odile had some of the tastes that I had condemned in poor Denise Aubry.

What did we talk about? I no longer remember. In my

diary I find: 'A walk with O. San Lorenzo. She described the great light that shone over her bed at the convent, which came through a shutter, lit up from a lamp outside. When falling asleep she saw it growing bigger and believed herself to be in Paradise. She talked about the Bibliotheque Rose; detested Camille and Madeleine; and couldn't bear to play the role of the good child. Her favourite books were fairy stories and poetry. She dreamed sometimes of walking under the sea and that skeletons of fish were swimming round her, also that a weasel was dragging her under the earth. She liked danger; and took the highest jumps when out riding . . . She had a pretty way of moving her eyes when trying to understand something – wrinkling her forehead a little and looking in front of her as though she could not quite see, then said to herself "Yes" – she had understood.'

I am well aware that I am powerless to describe the memories of happiness the thought of her evoke in me. Why did I experience a sense of perfection? Was there anything remarkable in what Odile said? I don't think so, but she possessed something that all the Marcenats lacked; a love of life.

We are drawn towards those who secrete a mysterious essence that our composition lacks and which we need in order to establish an equilibrium. I may not have known more beautiful women than Odile, I have certainly known more brilliant and intelligent ones, but none who could put the world of the senses within my reach as she did. Removed as I was by too much reading and too many solitary meditations, from trees, flowers, the scents of the earth, the beauty of the sky and the freshness of the air, I found all these things gathered each morning by Odile and placed by her in a sheaf at my feet.

When I was alone in a town I passed my time in museums

or in my room reading books about Venice or Rome. One might say that the exterior world reached me only through the medium of masterpieces. Odile drew me at once into the universe of colour and sound. She took me to the flower-market under the high arches of the Mercato Nuovo. She mingled with the housewives who were buying sprays of lilies of the valley or branches of lilac, and liked the old country parson who was bargaining over the price of laburnum wound round a long reed. On the hills above San Miniato she led me through narrow streets between over-heated walls from which hung thick clusters of wistaria.

Did I bore her in my serious Marcenat way, with descriptions of fights between Guelphs and Ghibbelines, the life of Dante or the economic situation in Italy? I don't think so. Who was it said that sometimes a few naïve, almost foolish words spoken by a woman give a man an irresistible desire to kiss her childish mouth, whereas it is often when a man is most serious and severely logical that a woman loves him best? Perhaps this was true of Odile and myself. In any case when she murmured beseechingly: 'Do let us stop' in passing an imitation jewellers shop, I did not criticise or deplore her taste; but thought only: 'How I love her,' and felt growing ever stronger, the theme of the protective Knight and of devotion until death – which since my childhood I had associated with the idea of true love.

Then everything in me took up this theme. As in an orchestra a single flute, outlining a short phrase, seems to awaken one after another the violins, 'cellos and brasses until an overpowering rhythmical wave unfolds itself, and flows through the hall; thus the gathered flower, the scent of wistaria, black and white churches, Botticelli and Michelangelo, join one by one in a blissful chorus to proclaim the joy of loving Odile and of protecting her perfect and fragile beauty from an invisible enemy.

The evening I arrived I longed for what then seemed an unattainable privilege, a two hours' walk with this unknown girl. A few days later I considered it intolerable slavery to be forced to return to the hotel for meals. Mme Malet, not knowing quite who I was, became uneasy and tried to slow down the progress of our intimacy, but the first awakening of love between two young people rouses forces which seem insuperable. We felt waves of sympathy forming round our path. Odile's beauty would have been enough, but she told me that as a couple we had even more success in that little Italian world than she had when alone. The Florentine shop-keepers were grateful to us for loving each other, the museum attendants smiled at us, even the boatmen on the Arno raised their heads complacently to watch us leaning on the parapet, so close together as to feel the warmth of each other's bodies.

I telegraphed to my father that I thought a week or two more in Florence would complete my cure and he agreed to the suggestion. I now wanted Odile with me all day. I hired a carriage and we went for long drives in the Tuscan country-side.

On the road to Siena we seemed to be passing through the background of one of Carpaccio's paintings. The carriage mounted the hillocks, which looked like children's sand castles, on the summit of which were unreal looking em-battled villages. The massive shadows of Siena enchanted us.

While lunching with Odile in a cool dark hotel I already knew that I should spend my life with her. During our return at night she put her hand in mine. That evening I wrote in my diary: 'Obvious sympathy with us shown by chauffeurs, maids and peasants. No doubt they see that we love each other. The art displayed by the people of that little hotel . . . It is wonderful how when we are together we disregard everything apart from ourselves. There is a delightful animation in her face, an expression of surrender and rapture combined with sadness, as if she wanted to gaze at the present moment and fix it for ever before her eyes.'

How I still love the Odile of those weeks in Florence! She was so beautiful that I almost doubted her reality. I turned my head away and said to her: 'I will try not to look at you for five minutes.' I could never hold out for more than thirty seconds. There was poetry in everything she said.

Although she was gay there was at times a sound like the low note of a 'cello in her voice, a melancholy discord that suddenly filled the air with some confused and tragic menace. What was the phrase she repeated at these moments?

'Fatally condemned . . .' that was it – 'under the influence of Mars, fatally condemned, girl with the golden hair, beware!' In what worthless novel or melodrama had she read or heard these words?

When one evening at twilight in a warm and hidden olive grove I kissed her for the first time, she looked at me sadly and said:

'You remember, darling, the words of Juliet?'

> In truth, fair Montague, I am too fond,
> And therefore thou mayst think my 'haviour light . . .

I think of our love at that time with great pleasure; it was as deeply felt by Odile as by me. But her feelings were nearly always restrained by pride. She explained to me later that first, life in the convent and afterwards with her mother, whom she did not love, had forced her to repress all emotions.

When this hidden fire appeared it was in brief and violent

outbursts which touched my heart all the more poignantly because they were involuntary. Just as certain past fashions by concealing woman's form lent charm to the mere touch of her garments, so do subtle phrases that disguise passionate sentiments enhance the beauty of language.

The day my father finally recalled me to Paris by a rather resentful telegram I had to announce the news to Odile at the Guardis, where she had arrived before I did. The people who were there, indifferent to my departure, resumed quite a remarkable conversation about Germany and Morocco. As we left I said to Odile:

'It was interesting what Guardi was saying!' She answered despairingly: 'I heard only one thing, that you are leaving.'

V

I was engaged when I left Florence. I had to inform my parents and thought with misgivings of how they would take the news. To the Marcenats, marriage was a family matter. My uncles would interfere and make enquiries about the Malets. What would they hear? I knew nothing about Odile's family and had not even met her father. I have told you about the Marcenat tradition, never to convey important news direct to the person concerned but through an intermediary, with endless precautions.

I begged my Aunt Cora, who was my favourite confidant, to tell my father of my engagement. She was always glad to prove the value of her information service, which was indeed remarkable, although it had the curious defect of being composed of agents too highly placed in the social hierarchy. Thus, if one wanted details about the life of a corporal Aunt

Cora could only obtain them from the War Minister or if about a doctor in Limoges, from the head surgeon in a Paris hospital.

When I mentioned M Malet she replied as I expected:

'I don't know him, but if he is anybody I shall find out at once from old Berteaux – you know – the architect who belongs to the Institute and whom I invite on two Tuesdays every winter because poor Adrien used to hunt with him.'

I saw her again a few days later and she seemed gloomy but agitated.

'My poor boy, it was lucky you consulted me. It is not a marriage for you. I saw old Berteaux who knows Malet very well, they shared rooms for the Prix de Rome. He says he's a nice man, had talent but is not a success because he has never done anything. He is the type of architect who is capable of making a design but never supervises the work and therefore loses his clients . . . I met that type when I built my villa at Trouville. I knew his wife when she was Mme Boehmer. Berteaux reminded me . . . Hortense Boehmer . . . this is her third husband. It appears that the daughter is, as you say, very beautiful and it is natural that she attracts you, but trust my experience my dear Philippe, don't marry her and don't speak of her to your father or mother . . . It is not the same for me, I have known so many people in my life, but your poor mother . . . I can't see her with Hortense Boehmer – Good Heavens, no!'

I told my aunt that Odile was quite different to her family, in any case my decision was made and it would be better if it were at once approved of at home. After slight resistance Aunt Cora consented to speak to my parents, partly out of kindness and partly because she resembled those old ambassadors who have a passion for negotiation and foresee a period of international difficulties, with fear because they want peace and with a secret pleasure because they will have an opportunity to exercise their only real talent.

My father was calm and indulgent and asked me to think it over. As for my mother, at first she was delighted at the prospect of my getting married but a few days later she met an old friend who knew the Malets and said their circle was very free and easy. Mme Malet had a bad reputation; she was supposed still to have lovers. Nothing precise was known about Odile but she had certainly been badly brought up, went out alone with young men and moreover was too pretty.

'Have they any money?' asked my Uncle Peter, who was of course present at the conversation.

'I don't know,' said my mother, 'it seems that this M Malet is an intelligent man, but rather odd. They are not our kind.'

This was a true Marcenat expression and a terrible indictment.

For several weeks I feared it would be very difficult to make them accept my marriage. Odile and her mother returned to Paris a fortnight after I did. I went to see them. The Malets lived in the rue Lafayette on the third floor. A door disguised as a panel led to M Malet's office and Odile took me in to him. I was accustomed to the orderly method my father exacted from his employees at Gandumas and at the rue de Valois; when I saw these three badly lighted rooms, the green half-torn portfolios and the sixty-year old draughtsman, I understood that my aunt's informant had been right in describing M Malet as an architect without work.

Odile's father was talkative and superficial; he received me almost too cordially, spoke of Florence and then about Odile in touchingly affectionate terms. He showed me drawings of villas he 'hoped' to build in Biarritz.

'I should very much like to design a large modern hotel in the Basque style. I submitted a plan for Hendaye, but didn't get the order.'

While he spoke I felt worried and apprehensive as to the impression he would make on my family.

Mme Malet invited me to dinner the next evening. I arrived at eight o'clock and found Odile alone with her brothers, M Malet was in his office reading and Mme Malet had not yet returned. The two boys, Jean and Marcel, were like Odile and yet from the first minute I knew we should never become intimate. They wanted to be friendly, even brotherly, but several times during the evening I caught them exchanging glances and making faces which clearly meant: 'He is not amusing . . .' Mme Malet came in at eight-thirty, without making excuses. Her husband appeared when he heard her, like a good boy, book in hand. As we sat down at table the maid announced a young American, a friend of the children's. He was not expected but was welcomed with shouts of joy.

In the midst of this confusion Odile retained the air of an indulgent goddess: seated beside me, she smiled at her brothers' jokes and when she saw that I was shocked, calmed them down.

She appeared to me as perfect as in Florence, but I suffered at seeing her in the midst of this family. I heard a muffled Marcenat refrain under the triumphant march of my love.

My parents visited M and Mme Malet and preserved an air of polite disapproval in spite of the enthusiastic reception they received. Fortunately my father being like me, very susceptible to feminine beauty, was captivated by Odile at once. On leaving he said to me:

'I don't think you are wise . . . but I understand.'

My mother said: 'She is certainly pretty; rather peculiar and says curious things; she will have to change herself.'

In Odile's eyes the most important meeting of all was between her best friend Misa and myself. I remember being nervous about it; I felt that Misa's opinion counted a great deal for Odile; however I quite liked her. She was not as beautiful as Odile but had grace and regular features. Compared with Odile she looked rustic but their faces seen together formed a pleasing contrast. I soon got into the habit of seeing them as a single picture and looking upon Misa as Odile's sister. But there was a natural refinement in Odile which made her very different from Misa although they belonged by birth to the same social environment.

At the concerts we went to every Sunday during our engagement I noticed how much more attentive Odile was to the music than Misa. Odile, her eyes closed, letting the music flow through her, seemed happy and forgetful of the world. Misa looked round curiously, recognised people, opened and read her programme and irritated me by her restlessness. She was a pleasant companion, always gay and contented and I was grateful to her for having told Odile that she thought me charming.

We spent our honeymoon in England and Scotland. I cannot remember a happier period than those two months of shared solitude. We often passed our days lying in flat shiny boats furnished with light cretonne cushions, and stopped in flower-decked hotels beside rivers and lakes. Odile opened my eyes to the country, fields of bluebells, beds of tulips, springy mown lawns and willow trees trailing their foliage on the water like a woman letting her hair down. I learned to know a new Odile, even more beautiful than the one in

Florence. To watch her live was an enchantment. The moment she entered an hotel room she transformed it into a work of art. She had a naïve and touching affection for the mementos of her childhood which she always took about with her; a little clock, a lace covered cushion and a volume of Shakespeare bound in grey suede. When our marriage broke up and she left me she still carried the lace cushion under her arm and the Shakespeare in her hand. She skimmed the surface of life, more like a spirit than a woman. I wish I could have painted her walking along the banks of the Thames or the Cam, with a step so light that she seemed to be dancing.

On our return Paris appeared absurd to us. My parents and Odile's thought that our one desire would be to see them. Aunt Cora wanted to arrange dinner parties in our honour. Odile's friends complained of her two months' absence and begged me to restore her to them sometimes, but we only wished to go on living by ourselves.

The first evening that we took possession of our home, the carpets were not yet laid and there was a smell of paint, Odile in a fit of joyful mischief went to the front door and cut the bell wire. Thus she dismissed the world.

We made a tour of our house and she asked me if she could have a little study for herself next to her room. 'It will be my corner . . . You will come in only if I invite you. You know I sometimes have a wild longing for independence Dickie.' (She called me Dickie ever since she heard a girl in England hail a young man by that name.) 'You don't know me yet, you will see I am terrible.'

She had brought some champagne, cakes and a bunch of asters. With a low table, two armchairs and a crystal vase she improvised a charming scene for our gay, light-hearted supper. We were alone and we loved each other.

I do not regret those fleeting moments. Their last harmonics, growing ever fainter, still linger in my ear.

VI

And yet it was as early as the day following that happy evening that the first shock occurred, which marked the transparent crystal surface of my love with a faint blemish. It was a small episode but a foretaste of what was to follow. We were at an upholsterer's ordering our furniture. Odile had chosen some curtains that I thought expensive. We argued a little, in a friendly way, then she gave in. The salesman, a good-looking young man, had taken my wife's part energetically and I was irritated. As we were going out I saw – in a mirror – a glance of understanding and regret exchanged between the two. I cannot describe what I felt. Since my engagement I had unconsciously acquired the absurd illusion that my wife's mind would thereafter be linked with mine, and by a permanent transfusion our thoughts would be the same. The idea that this woman living beside me should be independent was incredible and still more so was the possibility of her conspiring against me with a stranger. I could say nothing. I was not even certain that I had actually seen this fleeting glance, but from that moment the meaning of jealousy was revealed to me.

I had hitherto regarded it as a theatrical and contemptible sentiment. The tragic figure of jealousy was represented for me by Othello and the humorous one by Georges Dandin. The likelihood of my ever playing one or perhaps both of these parts was out of the question. I had always left my mistresses when I was tired of them. If they had been unfaithful I did not know it.

I remember replying to a friend who said he was suffering from jealousy: 'I do not understand you . . . I could not love a woman who had ceased to care for me.'

Why did I feel so uneasy when I saw Odile with her friends? She was sweet and good humoured but seemed to create an atmosphere of mystery around her. I had not noticed this while we were engaged or during our honeymoon. Then our solitude and the complete mingling of our lives left no room for mystery, but in Paris I sensed it at once, like a distant indefinable threat. We were united, tender, but I must admit that from the second month of our life together I knew that the Odile I had loved was not the real one. I loved the Odile I now discovered as much, but in a different way.

In Florence I believed I had found the Amazon; I had created a mythical and perfect Odile. I was mistaken. Odile was not the goddess I had invented; she was a woman, divided and complex. No doubt she now saw me as a very different person to her bemused lover of Florence.

On my return I had to occupy myself seriously with the factory at Gandumas and the Paris office. My father, absorbed by the Senate, had been overworked during my absence. The business quarter was a long way from the house we had rented in the rue de la Faisanderie. It was impossible for me to return home for lunch. I passed one day a week at Gandumas and as the hurried journey was too tiring for Odile we had to spend a great deal of our time apart.

When I came home in the evening I felt happy at the thought of seeing my wife's lovely face again. I liked the surroundings she had created for herself. I was not accustomed to live amongst beautiful things but I now seemed to have an innate need of them and Odile's taste delighted me. At my parents' home at Gandumas, furniture had been accumulated without art for three or four generations. It encumbered the rooms, some of which were hung with bluish-green tapestries, and crudely drawn peacocks wandered amongst the trees on stained glass. Odile had our walls painted in plain soft colours; she liked almost empty rooms with large open spaces covered with light carpets. When I entered her boudoir I had such a striking impression of beauty that I felt vaguely uneasy.

My wife lay on a sofa, nearly always in a white dress, beside her on the low table that we used for our first supper was a Venetian vase with a narrow neck holding a single flower and occasionally some delicate foliage.

I learned to follow the seasons through the florist's windows and when I brought home from the office a white paper cornet containing her favourite flowers, she would admire them rapturously. Then she would spend an hour looking for exactly the right vase to show the most graceful curve of the stalk of an iris or a rose.

But after that our evenings often became strangely sad, like those sunny days when heavy clouds descend and take the world by surprise. We had little to say to each other. I had often tried to talk to Odile of my business, but it did not interest her. She had now exhausted the novelty of hearing about my youth; I had no fresh ideas as I never had time to read. She was aware of this.

I tried to draw my two most intimate friends into our lives. André Halff displeased Odile at once; she thought him ironical, almost hostile and indeed he was so with her. I once said to him:

'You don't like Odile!'

'I think she is very beautiful,' he said.

'Yes, but not very intelligent?'

'That's true . . . it is not necessary for a woman to be intelligent.'

'Actually you are mistaken; Odile is very intelligent, but she has not your kind of intelligence; she is intuitive, realistic.'

'That's quite possible,' he said.

With Bertrand it was different. He had attempted to form a serious and confidential friendship with Odile and had found her resistant and on the defensive . . . Bertrand and I would willingly spend a whole evening together, smoking and reconstructing the universe. Odile preferred to end the day at theatres, night-clubs, or travelling fairs. One evening she made me wander about for three hours amongst stalls, performing horses and shooting galleries. Odile, with her two brothers, gay and a little crazy, was enjoying herself thoroughly. Towards midnight I said:

'Now Odile, haven't you had enough? You must admit it is rather ridiculous. Surely you cannot get much pleasure from throwing balls at bottles, whirling round in dummy cars and winning a gilded glass boat after forty turns?'

She replied with a phrase from a philosopher, that I had made her read:

'What does it matter if a pleasure be false so long as one believes it to be real . . .' and, taking her brother's arm, she ran off towards a shooting-gallery; she shot well and having knocked down ten eggs with ten shots came back in a good humour.

When we married I thought that Odile, like me, hated society. I was mistaken. She liked dinners and dances; as soon as she had discovered Aunt Cora's smart and lively group she wanted to go to the Avenue Marceau every Tuesday. My one wish was to have Odile to myself; I was only really at peace when I knew that her beauty was safely enclosed in the narrow circle of our home. I felt this so strongly that I was happier when Odile, always delicate, and often overcome by fatigue, had to stay in bed for some days. Then I sat the whole evening in an armchair by her bed; we had long conversations together that she called 'palavers' and I read to her. I soon learnt the type of books that could hold her attention for some hours. Her taste was not bad but a book had to be melancholy and passionate to please her. She liked 'Dominique', Turgenev's novels and some English poetry.

'It is strange,' I said to her, 'when one does not know you well you appear frivolous yet at heart you only like sad books.'

'But I am very serious, Dickie; perhaps that is why I am frivolous. I don't want to show myself to everyone as I really am.'

'Not even to me?'

'Yes – to you – Don't you remember Florence?'

'Yes, in Florence I knew you well. But now, darling, you are very different.'

'One need not always be the same.'

'You never say anything nice to me now.'

'One doesn't say nice things to order; be patient; they will come back . . .'

'Like in Florence?'

'But of course, Dickie, I have not changed.'

She held out her hand and I took it, then a 'palaver' started again about my relations, or hers, Misa, or a dress she was going to order, then about life. The evenings she was relaxed and tender she resembled the Odile myth I had created. Amiable and weak, she was in my power. I was grateful to her for this languor. As soon as she was stronger again and could go out she became once more the mysterious Odile.

She never told me, as many shallow and talkative women would have done, where she went and what she did in my absence. If I questioned her she answered in a few words, usually obscure. What she said never gave me a satisfactory idea of the sequence of events. I remember that later one of her friends said to me, with that hardness women can show towards each other: 'Odile is a mytho-maniac.'

It was untrue, but though I was indignant at the moment, afterwards when thinking it over I could see quite well what had given rise to this view of Odile. Her carelessness in the telling and indifference to accuracy . . .

When, surprised by an unlikely detail, I queried it, she became completely dumb like a child to whom an indiscreet master puts too difficult a question.

One day, when contrary to my habit, I had returned for lunch, Odile, at two o'clock, asked the maid for her hat and coat.

'What are you doing this afternoon?' I asked her.

'I have an appointment with the dentist.'

'Yes, darling, but I heard you telephoning; your appointment is not until three. What will you do till then?'

'Nothing, I like to go there slowly.'

'But, my child, that is absurd, the dentist lives in the rue Malakoff. You will be there in ten minutes and you have an hour. Where are you going?'

She answered: 'You amuse me,' and went out.

That evening after dinner I could not resist asking her:

'Well, what did you do between two and three?'

She tried at first to make a joke of it, then, as I insisted she got up and went to bed without saying goodnight. This had never happened before. I went to ask her forgiveness. She kissed me. When I saw that she was appeased, I asked her: 'Do be nice, tell me what did you do between two and three?'

She burst out laughing. But later during the night, hearing a sound I went to her room and found she was quietly crying. Why was she crying? From shame or vexation? In answer to my questions, she said:

'I love you. But take care: I am very proud . . . I am capable of leaving you, though I love you, after a few scenes like this . . . Perhaps I would be wrong, but you must take me as I am.'

'Darling, I will do my best, you too must try to change yourself a little: you say you are proud; can't you sometimes conquer your pride?'

She shook her head obstinately.

'No, I cannot change myself. You always say that you love my naturalness. If I changed I should stop being natural. It is for you to become different.'

'My darling, I could never change myself to the point of understanding what I do not understand. My father brought me up to respect above all truth and accuracy. It is second nature to me . . . No, I could never say sincerely that I understand what you did today between two and three.'

'Oh! I've had enough,' she said impatiently. And turning on her side she pretended to sleep.

The next day I expected to find her resentful, but, on the contrary, she welcomed me gaily as though everything had been forgotten. It was a Sunday. She asked me to go to a concert with her. They were playing 'L'Enchantement du Vendredi Saint' which we both liked very much. On leaving the concert she wanted me to take her to tea. Nothing was more touching than Odile when she was gay, glad to be alive; one felt so strongly she was made for joy, that it seemed criminal not to give it to her. Watching her on that Sunday, so animated, so brilliant, I could hardly believe in our quarrel of the night before. But the more I knew my wife the more I understood how easy it was for her to forget, like a child. Nothing was more opposed to my own nature and to my mind, which noted, accumulated and registered.

Life for Odile that day consisted of a cup of tea, well buttered toast and fresh cream. She smiled at me and I realised how far apart are people who only live in the present from those who live in the past.

I still felt unhappy but I could not bear her a grudge for long; I reproached myself, made resolutions, vowed I would not ask any more useless questions and would trust her. We walked home through the Tuilleries and the Champs-Elysées; Odile breathed in the fresh autumn air with delight. It seemed to me that, as in Florence, the russet trees, the grey and golden light, the joyous movement of Paris, children's boats with their sails bending over the big pond and the fountain playing in their midst, all sang in unison the theme of the Knight Errant.

I repeated to myself a sentence from the Imitation. It had always appealed to me and I formed the habit of applying it to my relationship with Odile: 'Here am I before you, like your slave, I am ready for whatever may befall since I desire nothing for myself, but only for you.'

When I succeeded thus in overcoming my pride and in humiliating myself, not before Odile, but more precisely before my love for Odile, I felt more at peace.

VII

The person Odile saw most of was Misa. They telephoned to each other every morning, sometimes talking for more than an hour, and went out together in the afternoons. I favoured this friendship as it occupied Odile harmlessly while I was at the office. I was even pleased to see Misa at our home on Sundays and several times when Odile and I were going away for two or three days it was I who suggested taking her friend with us.

I want to explain the feelings that guided me so that you will understand the strange part Misa played later in my life. First of all, if I still wished to be alone with Odile as in the first weeks of our marriage, it was more from a vague fear of what new acquaintances might bring into our lives than for the positive pleasure it gave me.

I did not love her less but I knew that exchange of thought between us would always be limited and that an attempt at deep and serious conversations would be received by her with diminishing goodwill. On the other hand it was true that I began to enjoy her rather crazy, frivolous, slightly sad but always pleasant chatter and those 'palavers' which were Odile's natural conversation. She was only really herself with Misa. When talking together they revealed a trivial aspect of their minds that amused and touched me because it showed what Odile must have been like as a child. I was delighted one evening when at an hotel in Dieppe they were arguing like children, Odile ended by throwing a pillow at Misa's head shouting:

'Horrid girl!'

I also had a disquieting feeling, that must often arise when a young woman is involved in a man's daily life by circumstances other than love. As a result of our journeys together and Odile's familiarity which encouraged mine, I became almost as intimate with Misa as with a mistress. One day when we were discussing women's physical strength she challenged me. We wrestled for a moment, I overthrew her, then got up feeling rather ashamed.

'What children you are!' said Odile.

Misa remained stretched on the floor for a long time, looking at me intently.

She was, moreover, the only human being Odile and I welcomed with equal pleasure. Halff and Bertrand no longer came often, which I did not much regret. I had got to feel the same about them as Odile did. Hearing her talk to them I felt as though I had a dual personality. Seeing her through their eyes I considered that she treated serious matters with unbecoming levity. Yet I preferred her foolish conversation to my friends' theoretical discussions. Thus I was ashamed of my wife before them and proud of her privately. When they went away I said to myself that in spite of everything Odile was their superior by reason of her more direct contact with life and with nature.

Odile did not like my family and I didn't much like hers. My mother wanted to advise her about the choice of furniture, her way of life and the duties of a young wife. Advice was the last thing Odile could tolerate. When speaking of my parents she adopted a tone that shocked me very much. I too was bored at Gandumas and thought the Marcenats sacrificed all the pleasure of life to a conformity that showed no evidence of a sacred origin. At the same time I was proud of the austerity of our family traditions. Life in Paris, where the Marcenats were nobodies, should have cured me of the mania of attributing so much importance to them, but just as certain small religious communities transported to savage continents see millions of men worshipping other gods, without their own faith being disturbed, so we Marcenats, transported to a pagan world retained the memory of our local eminence.

Even my father, who admired Odile, could not help being irritated by her. He was too kind and reserved to show it, but I who understood and had inherited his shyness knew how much Odile's manner must have offended him.

When my wife was in doubt or angry about anything she discussed it openly and violently and then forgot it. This was not how we had been taught human beings should behave to each other. When Odile said to me: 'Your mother came here in my absence and took it upon herself to make remarks to the servant; I am going to ring her up and tell her that I won't stand it . . .' I begged her to wait. 'Listen Odile, fundamentally you are right but don't try to tell her yourself, you will only upset her. Let me tell her, or better still, ask Aunt Cora to explain to my mother that you said . . .' Odile burst out laughing.

'You don't realise how funny your family is . . . but at the same time it is terrible – yes, Dickie, it is terrible, because I love you less when I see what caricatures of yourself all these people are . . . I know you are not like that by nature, but you bear their imprint.'

The first summer Odile and I spent together at Gandumas was rather painful. At home we lunched at twelve sharp and the idea of keeping my father waiting had never occurred to me. But Odile would take a book into the field or go for a walk by the stream and forget the time. My father was walking up and down in the library and I ran across the park to look for my wife; I came back breathless not having found her and then saw her arrive, smiling, calm, and pleased to have been basking in the sun. When, at the beginning of the meal, we remained silent to show disapproval which from a group of Marcenats could only be indirect and wordless, she looked at us with a defiant mocking smile.

At the Malets, where we dined once a week, the situation was just the reverse; it was I who felt myself observed and criticised. Meals there were not solemn ceremonies; Odile's brothers got up to fetch some bread; M Malet spoke of a passage he had read, did not succeed in quoting it correctly and in his turn went out to refer to a book. Conversation was extremely free; I disliked hearing M Malet speak of indecent subjects in front of his daughter. I knew how absurd it was to attach so much importance to such trifles. It was not a question of my passing judgement on them, but I could not help feeling distressed. I was not happy at the Malets; their atmosphere was not mine. I knew that I was being dull and boring and was ashamed of my silence but could not throw it off.

At the Malets, as at Gandumas, my uneasiness was only on the surface because I still had the great joy of watching Odile live. When I was placed opposite her at dinner I could not help looking at her. A warm luminous glow seemed to shine through her pale skin. At that time she nearly always wore white and at home surrounded herself with white flowers which suited her admirably. She was a strange combination of candour and mystery. I felt I was living beside a child, yet sometimes when she was talking to another man, I detected in her glance a vague reflection of an emotion hitherto unsuspected by me, and I seemed to hear the distant murmur of a wild and passionate people.

VIII

I have attempted to make you hear the opening passages of the themes (partly drowned by louder instruments) round which the unfinished symphony of my life has been constructed.

You have known the Knight Errant, the Cynic, and perhaps you remember the foolish story of the upholsterer that my scruples would not allow me to omit, and which first revealed to me the meaning of jealousy. You must be indulgent and try to understand. It is a painful effort to tell you the rest of the story. I wish to be completely open with you, all the more because I consider myself cured and intend to speak of my madness as objectively as a doctor who, having had an attack of delirium, forces himself to describe it. Some illnesses begin slowly and develop gradually; others break out violently with an acute attack of fever. Jealousy for me was a sudden, a terrible disease.

Now that I am calm and attempt to discover the causes of my illness, it seems to me they were many and various. First there was my great love and a natural desire to keep for myself even the smallest particles of that precious substance which was the essence of Odile; her words, her smiles and her glances. But this desire was not my only consideration, for when I had Odile to myself, if we were alone at home for instance, or if I took her away for a few days, she complained that I was far more concerned with my books or my thoughts than I was with her.

It was only when there was a possibility of others sharing her with me that I longed to keep her exclusively to myself. The cause of this sentiment must have been pride, which though masked by modesty and reserve was one of the dominating features of my father's family.

I wished to control and possess Odile's mind as I did the waters and forests, the long machines through which glided the paper pulp, the peasants' houses and the workmen's cottages in the Loue valley. I always wanted to know what was going on in her small head, under her curly hair, just as I knew every day from precise clearly written statements on pale blue paper, arriving from Limousin, exactly what was going on at the paper-mills.

I realise by the pain revived in me when dwelling on this particular point that the root of the trouble lay in my acute intellectual curiosity. I would not admit to myself that I did not understand Odile. Actually I believe she was impossible to understand and that no man who loved her could have lived with her without suffering. I even believe that had she been different I might never have known the meaning of jealousy. A man is not born jealous, he brings with him only a receptive condition that makes him liable to contract the disease, but Odile by her very nature and without intention constantly roused my suspicions.

The events of each day formed for me and my family a perfectly compact and definite pattern, provided they were accurately reported and described, but on passing through Odile's mind they became a misty and confused landscape. I cannot say that she deliberately distorted the truth. It was much more complex. For her, words and phrases had little meaning or value; she possessed the beauty of a dream-like figure and passed her life in a dream. I have told you that she lived almost entirely in the present moment. She invented a past and a future when she felt the need of them, then immediately forgot what she had invented. If she had wanted to deceive, she would have co-ordinated these things to give them at least an appearance of truth, but she never bothered to do this. She contradicted herself in the same sentence. Returning from a visit to the factory in Limousin, I asked her:

'What did you do on Sunday?'

'Sunday? I don't remember . . . Oh yes, I was very tired. I stayed in bed all day.'

Five minutes later, when we were talking of music, she suddenly exclaimed: 'Oh! I forgot to tell you; last Sunday I heard at a Concert that *Valse* by Ravel you told me about. I liked it so much . . .'

'But Odile, do you realise what you are saying? It is mad . . . surely you must know if you were at a concert or in bed on Sunday . . . you can't think I shall believe both things.'

'I don't ask you to believe them. When I am tired I say anything – I don't listen myself to what I say.'

'Now do try to remember accurately; what did you do last Sunday? Did you stay in bed or go to the concert?'

She remained confused for a moment, then said:

'I don't know any more – you make me lose my head when you behave like an inquisitor.'

I emerged from these conversations feeling very unhappy, uneasy, agitated, and unable to sleep. I spent hours trying to reconstruct from the lightest word she had let fall how she had really spent her day. I then reviewed in my mind all those disturbing friends whom I knew had filled Odile's life before our marriage. As far as Odile was concerned, it was as easy for her to forget such scenes as to forget anything else. In the morning I left her sulky and withdrawn, in the evening I found her joyful. I came in prepared to say to her: 'Listen darling, it's becoming impossible; we must think of separating.

I don't wish it, but if we are to live together you must make an effort, you must be different.'

I was welcomed by a girl in a new dress who kissed me and said:

'Misa telephoned, she has three seats for the theatre and we are going to see *A Doll's House* – and I in my loving weakness accepted this unlikely and reassuring fiction.

I was too proud to show that I was unhappy. My parents above all must not know it. Only two people during that first year appeared to have guessed what was happening. The first was my cousin Renée and this astonished me as we saw very little of her. She led an independent life which irritated our family quite as much as my marriage had done. While staying with my Uncle Peter at Vittel, where he took his yearly cure, she met a Paris doctor and his wife and became attached to them. She had always been rebellious and had grown hostile to the Marcenat principles. She made longer and longer visits to her new friends in Paris. Dr Prudhomme was rich and did not practise. He was engaged in cancer research and his wife helped him. Renée had inherited from her father, whom she resembled too closely to get on with, the taste for a task well done. She was soon adopted by the world of learned men and doctors into which her friends had introduced her. At twenty-one she demanded her dowry from her father and his permission to live in Paris. This caused a breach with her family for some months, but the Marcenats held too strongly to the fiction of indestructible love between parents and children to sustain the pretence of indifference for long.

When my Uncle Peter was convinced that his daughter's decision was final he gave way. From time to time he had bouts of anger, but they grew less frequent and he then implored her to get married. She refused and threatened never to set foot in Chardeuil again. In desperation my uncle and aunt promised to speak no more of marriage.

Renée came to our engagement party and sent Odile a lovely basket of white lilies. I remember this had surprised me; her parents had already given us a handsome present, why the flowers? A few months later we dined with her at my Uncle Peter's and invited her to come to us. She was very nice to Odile and interested me by accounts of her travels. Since I had given up seeing most of my old friends I hardly ever heard such sensible and well-informed conversation. When she was leaving I took her to the door:

'How pretty your wife is!' she said in sincere admiration.

Then she looked at me sadly and added: 'You are happy?' in a tone that suggested she did not believe I was.

The second one who lifted the veil for a moment was Misa. After a few months her attitude had become rather strange. It seemed to me that she was trying to be my friend rather than Odile's. One evening Odile was ill in bed. She had had two successive accidents and it was becoming unfortunately evident that she could not have children. Misa came to see her and sat down beside me on the sofa at the foot of the bed. We were very near to each other, almost hidden from Odile's eyes by the high wooden end of the bed; she could only see our heads. All at once Misa came still nearer, and pressing herself against me took my hand. I was so surprised that I still don't understand how it happened. Odile could see nothing from my face. I moved away with regret and that evening, taking Misa home, I kissed her lightly with a quick involuntary movement. She did not resist. I said:

'This is not right – poor Odile . . .'

'Oh – Odile!' she said, shrugging her shoulders.

That displeased me and afterwards I was very cold to Misa; but all the same, it worried me as I wondered if her 'Oh Odile!' meant 'Odile is not worth considering.'

IX

Two months later Misa was engaged. Odile said she could not understand her choice, and thought her fiancé Julien Godet very mediocre. He was a young engineer who had just left the Central School and, as M Malet said, 'had no position'. Misa seemed to be trying to love him, though she had not succeeded, but he was very much in love with her. My father had wanted for some time to find a manager for an auxiliary paper factory at Guichardie, near Gandumas; when he heard of Misa's marriage he thought of offering the post to her husband. I was not pleased at this project as I had lost confidence in Misa, but Odile liked being of service and giving pleasure and immediately told them of the offer.

'Take care, Odile, if you send Misa to live in Limousin you will miss her in Paris.'

'Yes, but I am doing it for her sake, not mine; and anyway I shall see her during those horrible visits to Gandumas, which will mean a lot to me and if she wants to come to Paris she can always stay with her parents or with us . . . the boy must do something and if we don't give him a job he will take her away to Grenoble or Castelnaudary.'

Misa and her husband accepted at once. Odile went to Gandumas in the middle of the winter to find them a house and asked the people in the district to visit them. One of Odile's qualities which I have not yet mentioned was her readiness to devote herself generously to her friends.

Misa's departure was a misfortune for our marriage as it had the immediate effect of throwing Odile back into a set that I disliked very much. Before our marriage she often went out alone with young men: they took her to the theatre; she also travelled with her brothers and their friends. She told me quite honestly about this when we were engaged and said she could not give it up. At that time I desired her more than anything in the world and had replied in good faith that I would never interfere with her friendships.

I had no idea when I made that promise what I should suffer at seeing another man greeted by Odile with the same welcoming look and smile I had loved so much. You may be surprised to hear of my distress at the second-rate quality of most of her friends. This should have reassured me; on the contrary I was mortified. When one loves one's wife as I did mine, everything associated with her is imbued with imaginary qualities and virtues and, just as the town in which we met seemed more beautiful than it really was, the restaurant where we dined together superior to all others, so even the detested rival may participate in the glamour we cast round our beloved. Of all the humiliations that a woman can inflict on us, the inferiority of our rival is the worst.

I should have been jealous but not surprised if I had found Odile surrounded by the most distinguished men of our time; I found her in the company of young men who, to judge impartially, were commonplace and certainly not good enough to associate with her. Moreover she had not even chosen them.

'Odile, why do you always try to attract men?' I asked her. 'I understand that an ugly woman wants to test her powers – but you . . . you have such an easy victory; it is cruel, darling, and disloyal. And your choice is so strange . . . For instance you are always seeing that Jean Bernier . . . what interest can he possibly have for you? He's ugly and vulgar.'

'He amuses me.'

'How can he amuse you? You are refined and have good taste. His jokes are the kind I have not heard since I was in the Army and the sort I would not dare to utter in your presence . . .'

'No doubt you are right; he is ugly, perhaps he is vulgar, although I don't think so, but I like seeing him.'

'But surely you are not in love with him?'

'Good gracious no! You are mad! I would not like him even to touch me, he gives me the impression of a slug . . .'

'Darling, you may not care about him, but I can see he is in love with you; you make two men unhappy, him and me.'

'You think everyone is in love with me. I am not as pretty as all that . . .'

She said this with such a charming smile that I relented and kissed her.

'Well then, darling, you will see less of him?'

She assumed her obstinate expression.

'I never said that.'

'You did not say so. But that is what I am asking you to do. What can it matter to you? It would please me and you say yourself that you are indifferent towards him . . .'

She seemed abashed, uncertain of herself, then said with an embarrassed smile: 'I don't know, Dickie, I can't very well help it . . . besides it amuses me.'

In saying these words Odile looked so childish and sincere. I then explained with my useless and terrible logic that it was easy to 'help it'.

'What destroys you,' I said, 'is that you accept yourself just as you are, as if our characters were ready-made, one can form one's character, one can remake it . . .'

'Then remake yours.'

'I am quite ready to try – but you must help me by trying too.'

'No, I have often told you that I can't. And I don't want to try,' she replied.

When I think of that far-off time I wonder if it was a deep instinct that inspired her attitude. If she had changed as I wanted her to, should I have continued to love her as much? Could I have endured the constant presence of that frivolous little creature if the tension of such scenes had not made boredom for either of us impossible? It was not true that she had never tried to change herself. Odile was not unkind. When she saw that I was unhappy she meant to do her best to comfort me, but her vanity and weakness were stronger than her good intentions and she remained the same.

I had learned to recognise what I called her 'look of triumph'; a heightened gaiety, her eyes were more brilliant, her beauty enhanced, and her usual languor had disappeared. When a man appealed to her I knew it before she did . . . At these times I thought of her words in Florence:

> In truth, fair Montague, I am too fond,
> And therefore thou mayst think my 'haviour light . . .

What saddens me most when I recall this unhappy period, as I often do, is the thought that in spite of her coquetry Odile was faithful to me and that perhaps, with a little more tact, I might have kept her love.

But it was not easy to know how to deal with her; she was bored by tenderness which produced in her irritable and hostile reactions; threats would have been useless. One of her most consistent traits was love of danger. Nothing pleased her more than being taken in a yacht in squally weather, driving a racing car over a difficult course, or riding over very high jumps. She went about with a crowd of reckless young men. Not one of them appeared more favoured than another and each time I happened to overhear their conversations it seemed to me that they were on terms of sporting comradeship. Besides, I have now come across letters written to Odile from these boys showing that she accepted a tone of amorous chaff which implied nothing more. One of them wrote to her:

'Strange Odile, so crazy and yet so chaste; too chaste to please me.'

And another, a sentimental and religious young Englishman, wrote:

'As it is certain, dear Odile, that you will never be mine in this world, I hope to be near you in the next.'

I am telling you things that I only knew much later, but at the time I could not believe in the innocence of this free manner of life.

To be fair I must add that at the beginning of our marriage Odile tried to include me in both her old and new friendships; she would willingly have shared all her friends with me. We met the Englishman during our first summer holiday in Biarritz; he amused Odile by giving her banjo lessons and singing negro songs. When he left he insisted on giving her the banjo, which annoyed me very much. A fortnight later she said:

'I have a letter from that little Douglas, in English, will you read it to me and help me to answer it?'

I do not know what possessed me: I told her with ill-concealed anger that I hoped she would not answer it, that

Douglas was an idiot and bored me . . . This was untrue; Douglas was charming, and had good manners. I should have liked him before my marriage. But I was getting into the habit of wondering what my wife was hiding whenever she spoke. Each time I found some obscurity in her remarks I concocted an ingenious theory to explain to myself why she was so mysterious. I felt a painful pleasure, almost a voluptuous suffering in believing that she was lying. My memory is usually poor but when it concerned Odile's stories it became astoundingly good. I remembered her lightest phrases, weighed them and compared them one with another: I once said to her:

'What? You have been to the tailor again? That makes the fourth fitting you have had for your suit. You went last Tuesday, Thursday and Saturday.'

She looked at me, smiled and without demur replied:

'You have a diabolical memory . . .'

I was ashamed of being fooled, and at the same time proud of seeing through her ruse. However my discoveries were useless; I did not do anything and did not wish to. Odile's mysterious calm manner gave me no opportunity to make a scene. I was both unhappy and passionately interested. I did not dare to take steps such as forbidding Odile to see certain of her friends, because I had discovered what ridiculous errors my desperate suspicions had caused me to make. For instance I remember that during several weeks she complained of headaches and tiredness and said she wanted to go to the country for a few days. I could not leave Paris at that moment and for a long time would not let her go; I did not realise my selfishness in refusing to believe she was ill. At last it occurred to me that it would be more ingenious to let her go to Chantilly as she wished and surprise her there the next evening. If I found someone with her, as I fully expected, I should at least know something definite and could leave her, which I imagined I wished to do – but it was not true.

The day after she left I hired a car, anticipating a scene, that I did not want my chauffeur to witness. I left for Chantilly after dinner. About halfway there I told the chauffeur to turn back to Paris, then, after going three kilometres, feeling madly impatient, I made him turn again towards Chantilly. At the hotel I asked the number of Odile's room. They did not want to give it to me. The reason seemed obvious. I showed my papers and proved I was her husband; at last a page boy took me up. I found her alone, surrounded by books and innumerable letters she had written. But had she not had time to organise this setting?

'What lengths you go to!' she said, pityingly. 'What did you expect? What are you afraid of? Did you think I might be with a man? What should I want to do with a man? You don't understand that I like being alone, just to be alone and, if you wish me to be quite frank, I want more than anything else not to see you for a few days. You tire me with your fears and suspicions. I have to watch my words and be careful not to contradict myself, like a prisoner in the witness box . . . I have spent a delightful day here, I have read, dreamed, slept, and been for a walk in the forest. Tomorrow I shall go to the chateau and look at some miniatures . . . It is all so simple if you only knew.'

But I was already thinking that after this success she would be able to send for her lover next time without fear.

Oh that lover of Odile's, how I tried to discover what sort of a man he was. I sought him in all that was inexplicable in my wife's mind and words. I had become incredibly shrewd in my analysis of her remarks: when she expressed ideas rather more subtle than usual, I suspected she had the unknown lover in mind.

A strange relationship developed between us. I admitted all my thoughts concerning her, even the harshest. She listened with patient indulgence, slightly irritated but flattered to be the object of so much curiosity and interest.

She continued to be ailing and went to bed very early. I spent nearly every evening at her bedside – strange and rather peaceful evenings. I explained the defects in her character while she listened, smiling, then held out her hand and, taking mine, said:

'Poor Dickie, how you torment yourself for a poor unhappy little girl who is naughty, stupid, vain and coquettish . . . for I am all that, am I not?'

'You are not stupid; you are not very intelligent . . . but you have surprising intuition and very good taste.'

'Ah – so I have good taste . . . then I still have something. Listen, Dickie, I am going to read you some English verses I have discovered and adore.'

She had a naturally refined taste and it was seldom that she liked anything second-rate, but even in her choice of verses I noticed with uneasy astonishment the feeling for love, a deep knowledge of passion and sometimes the desire for death. I remember above all a verse of Swinburne's that she often recited:

From too much love of living,
From hope and fear set free,
We thank with brief thanksgiving,
Whatever Gods may be,
That no life lives for ever,
That dead men rise up never,
That even the weariest river
Winds somewhere safe to sea.

'The weariest river . . .' she repeated again and again.

'I like that . . . it is me, Dickie, the weariest river . . . and I am going quietly towards the sea.'

'What nonsense – you are life itself.'

'Oh I look like that,' she said and then with a humorous sad grimace, 'but I am a very weary river.'

Before I left her that evening, I said: 'After all, Odile, with all your faults I really love you.'

'And I too, Dickie,' she replied.

X

For a long time my father had been asking me to go to Sweden on business for the paper-works as he was no longer well enough to travel himself.

I refused to go unless Odile accompanied me and she was not at all enthusiastic. This seemed to me suspicious. She liked travelling. I suggested that if she did not want to cross Germany and Denmark by train we could go by boat from Havre or Boulogne, which she would enjoy.

'No,' she said, 'go by yourself; Sweden doesn't attract me, it's too cold.'

'But that isn't true Odile, it is a delightful country . . . scenery that would appeal to you, solitude, big lakes surrounded by fir trees, old castles . . .'

'You think so? No. I don't want to leave Paris at present . . . But as your father wishes you to go do so by all means – it will be good for you to see other women besides me. Swedish women are enchanting, tall, pale blondes – just your type . . . Be unfaithful to me . . .'

In the end it was impossible to avoid the trip. I confessed

to Odile that I dreaded the thought of leaving her alone in Paris.

'How funny you are,' she said, 'I shan't go out I promise you; I have lots of books to read and I shall have all my meals with mother.'

I left feeling anxious and the first three days I was wretched. During the long journey from Paris to Hamburg I pictured Odile in her boudoir receiving a man whose face I could not see, playing all the music she loved on the piano. I imagined her smiling and animated, her face beautified by the happy expression that had formerly been reserved for me and which I had wanted to grasp, imprison and keep for myself alone. Which of her favourite friends had induced her to stay in Paris? Was it that idiot Bernier? Or that American friend of her brothers' – Lansdale?

At Malmö the newly varnished train and the novelty of the colours at last distracted me from my ceaseless brooding.

At Stockholm I received a letter from Odile. Her letters were strange; she wrote like a little girl:

> I am very quiet. I'm doing nothing. It is raining. I am reading. I have re-read *War and Peace*. I had lunch with mother. Your mother came here.

And so on, in short sentences that evoked nothing but for some reason, perhaps because of their emptiness and naïve simplicity, had a reassuring effect on me.

The following days only added to this feeling of relaxation. It was curious; I loved Odile more than when I was in Paris. I imagined her serious, rather languid, lying down and reading near a vase in which, no doubt, was a beautiful carnation or a rose. I was very lucid in spite of my madness and said to myself: 'How is it that I am not suffering? I ought to be unhappy. I know nothing about her. She is free and writes what she pleases.'

I realised that absence, though it favours the crystallisation of love, puts jealousy to sleep for a while by removing from the mind the small facts and observations on which its terrible and dangerous edifice is habitually built, thus forcing calmness and repose upon it.

Business obliged me to travel in the Swedish countryside; I stayed with the owners of large forests: I was offered the liqueurs of the country, with caviare and smoked salmon. The women had a cold brilliance; I succeeded in passing whole days without thinking of Odile and her doings.

I especially remember one evening after dining in the country near Stockholm, my hostess suggested a walk in the park. We were wrapped up in furs. The air was freezing. Tall fair menservants opened a wrought-iron gate and we found ourselves by the borders of a frozen lake that shone faintly in the midnight sun. The woman who accompanied me was charming and gay; a few minutes earlier she had played some preludes with a delicate grace that brought tears to my eyes. For a moment I experienced a feeling of extraordinary happiness. 'How beautiful the world is,' I thought, 'and how easy it is to be happy.'

My return to Paris revived my fears. Odile's description of her long days of solitude was so bare that I had to conjure up the most painful images to fill in the blank spaces.

'What have you been doing all this time?'

'Well, nothing. I rested, dreamed, and read –'

'What did you read?'

'I wrote to you – *War and Peace*.'

'But you did not spend a fortnight in re-reading a novel!'

'No, I did various things; I arranged my drawers,

tidied my books, answered old letters, went to dressmakers.'

'But who did you see?'

'Nobody. I told you in my letters; your mother and mine, my brothers, Misa . . and I played the piano a lot.'

She grew a little more lively as she talked of Spanish music, of Albeniz and Granados whom she had just discovered.

'And then, Dickie, I must take you to hear *The Sorcerer's Apprentice*. It is so clever.'

'Is it based on the story of Goethe's ballad?'

'Yes,' said Odile animatedly.

I looked at her. How did she know that ballad? I was sure she had never read Goethe. With whom had she been to the concert? She read the uneasy expression in my face.

'It was in the programme,' she said.

XI

The Tuesday after my return from Sweden we dined with Aunt Cora. She invited us twice a month and was the only member of my family with whom Odile had any sympathy.

Aunt Cora regarded Odile as a charming ornament to a party and was very kind to her but reproached me for having grown silent since my marriage. 'You are dull,' she said, 'and take too much notice of your wife; married couples are only possible at a dinner when they have reached the stage of indifference. Odile is delightful but you will be no use for the next two or three years; however, tonight as you have just returned from Sweden I hope you will be brilliant.'

Actually the success of the evening was not mine but François de Crozant's, a lieutenant in the Navy who had been stationed in the Far East. He was a friend of André Halff who talked of him with an odd mixture of fear, esteem and irony. He had been introduced to Aunt Cora by Admiral Garnier, the Naval Chief of Staff. That evening Crozant described the scenery of Japan and spoke of Conrad and Gauguin with a vivacious, poetic feeling which I could not help admiring, though I did not like him. As I listened I gradually remembered details André had told me about him in the past. He had been to the East several times and had a small house near Toulon, full of objects he had brought back from his travels. He composed music and had written a strange opera on an episode from Chinese history, and was well-known in sporting circles for having beaten several motor-racing records. He was one of the first naval officers to fly a hydroplane.

A man in love is extremely sensitive to the impression made on his beloved by others. Without being able to see Odile, who was at the other end of the table on the same side as I was, I knew exactly how she was looking and with what intense interest she must be listening to François' stories. My feelings resembled those of a father who has unwittingly exposed his cherished only daughter to a terrible epidemic and is hoping despairingly to save her from contamination by deadly germs. If only I could prevent Odile being in the same group as François after dinner, I might get her away at midnight free of infection. I had this good fortune though not by any action on my part, as François was taken immediately after dinner by Hélène de Thianges into the Chinese sitting room, reserved by Aunt Cora for couples who sought privacy. During this time I had a conversation about him with a pretty woman, Yvonne Prévost, whose husband was a captain in the Navy, assistant to the Admiral at the Ministry.

'Crozant interests you?' she said . . . 'I knew him well when I was a girl at Toulon where my father was Commander-in-Chief. Men thought Crozant superficial, some even called him disloyal, but women ran after him . . . I was too young to know but I heard what was said.'

'Tell me more about him.'

'I don't remember very well; I think he was vain; he seemed to fall passionately in love with a woman, overwhelm her with letters and flowers, then suddenly throw her over and begin to pay attention to someone else, without any explanation. He had a great deal of self-discipline, went to bed every night at ten o'clock when he wanted to keep fit, and even the prettiest women imaginable would be turned out when the hour struck . . . In love he was hard and cruel and assumed that it was a game of no more importance to others than to himself. You can imagine how he made women suffer.'

'Yes – I understand. But why did they love him?'

'Oh well – you know how it is . . . I had a friend who adored him; she said: "It was terrible, for a long time I could not get over it. He was so complex; irresistible and exacting, sometimes dry and brutal and at others tender and almost humble . . . It took me several months to discover that he could bring me nothing but misery." '

'Did she escape from him?'

'Yes – indeed she did – now she talks of him with indifference.'

'Do you think he is trying to cast his spell on Hélène de Thianges?'

'I'm sure he is but in this case he has an opponent who can stand up to him. A young woman like her with a good social position must be careful. François ruins women's reputations as he cannot help talking about his love affairs to everyone. At Toulon, when he had made a new conquest the whole town knew about it the next day.'

'What an odious man he must be!'

'Oh no,' she said, 'he has a lot of charm . . . only he is like that.'

We are nearly always the initial cause of our own undoing. I had been wise when I had decided not to speak of François to Odile. Why did I tell her of my conversation with Yvonne Prévost on the way home? I think I was unable to resist the pleasure of interesting Odile and watching her listen to me with lively attention. Perhaps too I had the illusion that such severe criticism of François might put her off him for ever.

'And you say he is a composer?' asked Odile when I had finished.

I had foolishly evoked the devil and it was now too late to rid myself of him. The rest of the evening I told her all I knew about François and his strange way of life.

'He must be interesting. Wouldn't you like to invite him sometime?' she said, with apparent indifference.

'Certainly, if we meet him again, but he is returning to Toulon. Did you like him?'

'No, I don't like the way he has of looking at women as though he can see through them.'

A fortnight later we met him again at Aunt Cora's; I asked him if he had left the Navy.

'No,' he said in his brusque and almost insolent manner, 'I am doing a six months' course in the hydrographic service.'

This time he had a long conversation with Odile; I can still see them seated on the same tapestry sofa, leaning towards each other and talking with animation.

During our return Odile was rather silent.

'Well,' I said, 'what do you think of my sailor?'

'He is interesting,' she answered, and did not speak again until we got home.

XII

On several Tuesdays in succession François and Odile took refuge in Aunt Cora's Chinese boudoir immediately after dinner. I suffered acutely, but was determined not to show it. I could not resist talking about François to other women in the hope of being able to tell Odile that they thought nothing of him, but they nearly all admired him. Even Hélène de Thianges who was considered sensible and whom Odile called Minerva on account of her wisdom, said:

'I assure you he is very fascinating.'

'In what way? I try to be interested in what he says but he always repeats the same thing, China, the conquering races, "intense" life, Gauguin and so on. When I first heard him talk I thought him remarkable, but later I realised it was a turn, and that hearing it once was quite enough.'

'Perhaps. You are partly right. But he tells such marvellous stories! Women are grown-up children, Marcenat; they have kept their sense of wonderment and the framework of their actual life is so limited, they always long to escape. You don't know how boring it is to be concerned every day with a house, cooking, guests and children! Married men and Parisian bachelors are all part of the domestic social machine and bring nothing new or fresh, whereas a sailor like Crozant appears like a being from another world.'

'But don't you think his false romanticism unbearable? I detest his adventures . . . they are obviously invented.'

'Which ones?'

'Oh, you know: There is one about the English girl in Honolulu throwing herself into the water after he left; then the Russian woman who sent him her photograph framed in a strand of her hair. I think they are in very bad taste.'

'I don't know those stories . . . Who told them to you? Odile?'

'No, everyone – why should it be Odile? Tell me honestly – don't you think them objectionable?'

'Maybe . . . All the same his eyes are unforgettable. Besides what you say is not quite true. You see him as a legendary figure, just talk to him and you will find he is very simple.'

When we met Admiral Garnier at Aunt Cora's one evening I contrived to talk to him alone and questioned him about Crozant.

'He is a real sailor,' he said, 'one of our future great commanders.'

I resolved to fight against my repulsion for Crozant, to see more of him and try to judge him impartially. When I first knew him with Halff he had shown rather a contempt for me and gave me the same unpleasant impression the first evening we renewed our acquaintance. But for several days now he seemed to be trying to overcome the boredom inspired by my ill-mannered, hostile silences. I concluded that he was interested in me on account of Odile and this did not make me like him any better.

I asked him to dine with us and wanted to think well of him but could not. He was intelligent, though fundamentally timid, and tried to disguise his timidity by asserting himself in an aggressive way that irritated me. He appeared to me much less remarkable than my old friends André and Bertrand and I could not understand why Odile, who had dismissed them so contemptuously, took such an interest in everything he had to say. From the moment he arrived she was transformed and became even prettier than usual. One day François and I had a discussion about love in her presence. I had said that the only thing that makes love a really beautiful sentiment is fidelity – fidelity at all costs until death. Odile glanced at François in a peculiar way, I thought.

'I don't see the great importance of fidelity,' he said, with his incisive diction which gave a metallic sound and an abstract meaning to his utterance, 'what matters is to live in the present, to extract from every moment the most intense emotion it can yield. This can be obtained only in three ways, by power, danger or desire. Why keep up the fiction of a desire that no longer exists by being faithful to it?'

'Because there is only real intensity in that which is enduring and difficult. Don't you remember the passage in Rousseau's *Confessions* when he says that to touch the dress of a chaste woman gives more delight than to possess a woman of easy virtue?'

'Rousseau was a sick man,' said François.

'I hate Rousseau,' said Odile.

Finding they were united against me I began to defend Rousseau, whom I disliked, with a clumsy vehemence and we all three understood that henceforth any discussion between us could become personal and hostile.

Several times when talking of his profession François interested me so keenly that I forgot my animosity for a few minutes. As he walked across the drawing-room after dinner, with his sailor's rolling gait, he said:

'Do you know, Marcenat, how I spent yesterday evening? Studying Nelson's battles in Admiral Mahan's old book.'

In spite of myself I experienced the same shock of pleasure that I had felt formerly on the arrival of André Halff or Bertrand.

'Really?' I replied. 'But is that because you like it or because you think it may be useful to you? Naval methods must have changed so much. All those stories of boarding ships, of favourable winds and positions to be taken up for firing a broadside – surely have no value nowadays?'

'Don't believe it,' said François, 'the qualities which gain victory on land, or at sea, are the same today as in the time of Hannibal or Caesar. Take Aboukir for instance . . . What was the secret of the English success? . . . First of all the tenacity of Nelson who, having searched in vain for the French fleet all over the Mediterranean, did not give up the pursuit, then the promptitude of his decision when he eventually discovered the enemy at anchor, and the wind favourable. Do you think these fundamental qualities of tenacity and courage cease to be valuable because a Dreadnought has replaced the *Victory*? Not at all, and in any case the essential principles of strategy are unalterable. Wait a moment – look –'

He took a pencil and paper from his pocket.

'Here are the two fleets . . . this arrow is the direction of the wind . . . these shadings the deep water . . .'

I leaned over him. Odile was seated at the same table, her chin resting on her hands; she was admiring him and from time to time watched me from under her long eyelashes. Would she listen like that to me, I asked myself, if I were describing a battle?

During François' visits Odile often related anecdotes and expressed quite brilliantly ideas that she had learnt from me when we were engaged. She had never referred to them and I thought they had been forgotten, but now my modest knowledge was paraded to impress another man with the masculine clarity of Odile's intelligence. The same thing had happened with Denise Aubry; often when we make a great effort to form a person's mind our work is used for the benefit of another.

Strangely enough the beginning of a real liaison between François and Odile must have coincided with what I thought was a period of relative security for me. Having compromised themselves for some weeks quite openly in my eyes and in those of all our friends, they had now become extraordinarily prudent, were seldom seen together and were never to be found in the same group at parties. Odile did not speak of him and if another woman mentioned his name she responded so casually that even I was taken in for a time. As Odile said, I had diabolical intuitions where she was concerned and the reason for this new attitude gradually became clear to me. I began to suspect that just because they met freely in private, they could keep apart in the evenings and appear to have hardly anything to say to each other.

I had formed the habit of analysing Odile's remarks with uncanny insight and discovered François hidden in her every phrase. I knew that he had become on friendly terms with Anatole France and went to see him at Villa Said on Sunday mornings. For some weeks Odile had been telling interesting and personal stories about France. One evening as we were leaving the Thianges where, although habitually silent and modest, she had astonished our friends by commenting with gusto on France's political ideas, I said: 'How brilliant you were, darling! You have never spoken about these things before – how did you know them?'

'Was I brilliant?' she said, pleased and yet uneasy, 'I did not notice it.'

'It is not a crime, you need not defend yourself. They thought you very intelligent . . . Who taught you all that?'

'I don't remember . . . It was someone at a tea-party the other day, who knows France.'

'Who was it?'

'Oh, I forget . . . I didn't think it was important.'

How clumsy Odile was! She wanted to preserve her usual manner and say nothing compromising and yet her new love emerged in every word she uttered. It made me think of flooded fields that appear normal, the grass looking firm and upright, whereas each step reveals the treacherous sheet of water that is already soaking into the earth. Although careful to avoid obvious pitfalls, such as actually mentioning François de Crozant, she was unaware of the indirect signs breaking through her conversation which displayed his name to all eyes as clearly as if it had been written in illuminated letters. Knowing Odile's tastes, ideas and beliefs so well, it was easy, interesting but very distressing for me to notice the rapid changes in her.

Without being very pious she had always been a believer and went to church every Sunday. Now she said: 'I am a Greek of the fourth century B.C. – I am a pagan.'

These phrases were indisputably an echo of François. She also said: 'Life – what is it? Forty miserable years that we live on a patch of mud. Why should one waste a moment of it in useless boredom?'

'François' philosophy – and what a crude one.' Sometimes I needed a moment's reflection to perceive the connection between her new and surprising interests and their source. For instance, she, who never read a newspaper, saw a headline:

'Forest fire in the south of France,' and snatched the sheet from my hands.

'Are you interested in forest fires, Odile?'

'No,' she said, giving me back the paper, 'I just wanted to know where it was.'

Then I remembered that François owned a little house in the midst of pinewoods at Beauvallon.

Odile, like a child playing at hunt-the-thimble and seen hiding it by everyone, was almost touching in her naïve precautions. When she reported a fact she had heard from one of her friends or our relatives she always named her informer, but when it came from François she said: 'I was told' or 'someone told me'.

She began to show an astonishing knowledge of naval affairs. She said we were going to have a new and faster cruiser, or a new type of submarine, or that the English fleet was coming to Toulon. People were astounded – 'It is not in the newspapers . . .' Odile alarmed, feeling she had talked too much, tried to modify her statement:

'Oh! I don't know . . . perhaps it isn't true.' But it was always true.

Her whole vocabulary was derived from François. His repertoire which had made me say that his conversation was a showpiece was repeated in turn by Odile. She spoke of 'intense life', the 'joys of conquest' and even of Indo-China. But in passing through her shadowy mind François' definite themes lost their clear outlines, as a river flowing into a lake loses the rigid framework of its banks, and is no more than a vague shadow eaten away and enveloped by small waves.

XIII

All this evidence proved without doubt that if Odile was not François' mistress, she was certainly meeting him secretly and yet I could not bring myself to force an explanation from her. What would be the use? I would point out to Odile many fine shades and endless verbal implications that my implacable memory had registered. She would burst out laughing, look at me tenderly and say:

'You amuse me!'

How should I answer? Could I threaten her? Did I want to break off our marriage? And moreover, in spite of appearances I might be mistaken. When I was honest with myself I knew quite well that my fears were justified but the thought made my life so unbearable, that I clung to an improbable hope.

Odile's behaviour and her secret thoughts became an obsession which never left me. At my office I could not work and passed whole days with my head in my hands dreaming and meditating; I could not sleep till three or four in the morning, brooding over problems to which I saw the solution only too clearly.

Summer came. François' course ended and he returned to Toulon. Odile seemed quite calm and not at all sad, which slightly reassured me. I did not know if he wrote to her; I saw no letters and the disquieting undertones in Odile's conversation occurred more rarely.

I had to go for my holiday in August as my father was going in July, but as Odile had been unwell most of the winter it was agreed that she should spend July at the Villa Choin in Trouville. A fortnight before the date arranged for her to leave, she said:

'If you don't mind I would rather not stay with Aunt Cora, I should prefer a quieter place. I detest the Normandy coast; there are too many people, especially in that house . . .'

'What, Odile! So now you are afraid of people, you always reproached me for avoiding them.'

'It depends on one's state of mind. At present I need peace and solitude . . . Don't you think I could find some little place in Brittany? I don't know it at all and everyone says it is so beautiful.'

'Yes darling, it is very beautiful, but it is too far for me to go and see you on Sundays as I could at Trouville. In any case you would have Aunt Cora's villa to yourself as she will not be there till August . . .'

Odile was evidently determined to go to Brittany and gently but persistently returned to the subject until I gave in. I was puzzled. I had expected her to suggest going near Toulon; that would have appeared natural as the summer had been bad and everyone was complaining of the dampness of Normandy. Although I was sad to part with her I felt a certain satisfaction that she was going in the opposite direction to François. She was particularly loving the day I saw her off at the station and on the platform kissed me saying:

'Don't be dull, Dickie, enjoy yourself . . . why not go out with Misa, she would be pleased.'

'But Misa is at Gandumas.'

'No, she will be in Paris at her parents' flat all next week.'

'When you are not there I don't want to go out. I stay at home by myself, feeling miserable.'

'You ought not to,' she said, as she stroked my cheek with a motherly gesture. 'I don't deserve to be thought about so much. I'm not interesting . . . You take life too seriously, Dickie. It is only a game.'

'Not a very amusing one.'

'No,' she said, and this time there was a trace of melancholy in her voice, 'it is not a pleasant game. Above all it is difficult. One does things one doesn't want to do . . . I think it is time to get into the train . . . Goodbye Dickie . . . You'll be all right.'

She kissed me again and as she mounted the steps gave me one of those radiant smiles that bewitched me and disappeared into the compartment. She hated last-minute farewells and affectionate demonstrations. Misa, later on, told me she was hard, but this was not true. She was capable of kind and generous impulses and because she was afraid of making any sacrifice by yielding to pity, she resisted it. It was then that her face assumed that obstinate and impenetrable expression which alone could make her ugly.

XIV

The next evening was a Tuesday and I dined at Aunt Cora's.

I was seated next to Admiral Garnier who spoke of the weather and a storm that had flooded Paris in the late afternoon.

He said, 'By the way I have just got a temporary post at Brest for your friend François de Crozant; he wanted to study the coast of Brittany.'

'At Brest?'

The glasses and flowers revolved in front of my eyes and I thought I was going to faint. Social instinct is so strong in us that we could almost assume indifference at the point of death.

'Really?' I said to the Admiral, 'I didn't know . . . when was this?'

'A few days ago.'

I talked to him about Vauban, about the port of Brest, its value as a naval base and its old houses. My thoughts were running on two distinct planes. On the surface, correct and banal sentences formed themselves, giving the admiral the impression of a normal person, enjoying the freshness of the evening. At a deeper level, an inner voice kept repeating: 'So that was why Odile wanted to go to Brittany.' I imagined her walking in the streets of Brest, leaning on François' arm with that radiant air I knew and loved so well. Perhaps she would stay a night with him. Morgat, the place she had chosen, was not far away from Brest. François might join her at the seaside? He is sure to have a motor-boat! They would explore the rocks together. Odile could make nature seem more beautiful on such an occasion.

I was astonished to find that knowing the truth at last gave me keen intellectual pleasure in spite of my intense suffering. Whenever Odile's actions were doubtful, I set myself the most painful and insoluble problems, but this time, when she had suggested going to Brittany, the explanation had occurred to me with startling clarity: 'François is there already!' Well he was there and though my heart was shattered, my mind was almost relieved.

On returning home I passed a whole night wondering what to do. Take the train to Brittany? No doubt I would find Odile on a little beach calm and happy; I should appear mad and would not even be reassured as I should think at once that François had already been and gone, which would be quite likely. The terrible part of the situation was that each fact relating to it could be unfavourably interpreted, therefore no remedy for my suffering seemed possible.

'Must I leave Odile? Shall I ever be at peace with her? Will she do nothing to spare me? We have no children; divorce would be easy.'

I thought of the period before I had known her. In those days my life lacked richness and grace, but it was at least normal and calm. Yet I knew that to live without Odile was inconceivable.

I turned over, tried to get to sleep by counting sheep or picturing landscapes. Nothing can help when the mind is obsessed. There were moments when I was furious with myself: 'Why do I still love her? Odile has some serious faults. She doesn't speak the truth, which I hate more than anything in the world. Why can't I free myself, shake off this bondage?' And I repeated: 'I don't love her.' But I knew it was untrue and that I loved her as much as ever without understanding the reason. At other moments I reproached myself for letting her go away. Should I have been able to prevent her? She had appeared to be carried away by a powerful and fatal emotion. Fleeting images of heroines of Greek tragedy entered my mind. I felt that she regretted what she was doing and yet could not help it. That day if I had lain down across a railway line she would have passed over my body without pity, to rejoin François.

Towards morning I tried to persuade myself that Odile's decision to go to Brittany might be a coincidence and perhaps she was even unaware of François' presence so near her. But I knew this was false. I went to sleep at dawn and dreamt I was walking in a Paris street near the Palais Bourbon. It was lit by an old-fashioned street-lamp. Seeing a man hurrying away from me, I recognised François' back, drew a revolver from my pocket and shot him. He fell. I was relieved and ashamed, and then woke up.

After two days I received a letter from Odile:

It is fine. The rocks are beautiful. I have met an old lady at the hotel who knows you; her name is Mme Jouhan; she has a house near Gandumas. I bathe every day. The water is warm. I have been for excursions in the countryside. I like Brittany very much. I have been out in a boat. I hope you are not unhappy. Are you enjoying yourself? Did you dine at Aunt Cora's last Tuesday? Have you seen Misa?

It finished with: 'I love you very much. I kiss you my darling.'

The writing was a little larger than usual. One could see that she wanted to fill up four pages so as not to hurt me, but found it difficult. 'She was in a hurry,' I thought, 'he was waiting for her'; she had said to him! 'I really must write to my husband.' Imagining my wife's face when she said these words I could not help thinking it beautiful and only wished for her return.

XV

The week following Odile's departure Misa telephoned to me:

'I know you are alone – Odile has deserted you. I'm alone too. I came to do some shopping and to have a glimpse of Paris and am staying at my parents' flat, but they are away. Do come and see me.'

I thought a talk with Misa might help me to forget for a while the terrible thoughts I was struggling with, so I agreed to go and see her that evening.

She opened the door to me as the maids were out, and looked pretty wearing a pink silk négligée copied from one of Odile's. Her hair was done differently, in the same style as Odile's.

The evening was chilly and Misa had lighted a wood fire. We sat before it on a pile of cushions, and began talking of our families, Gandumas, her husband and of Odile.

She asked: 'Have you any news of her? She hasn't written to me. It is unkind of her.'

I told Misa I had received two letters.

'Has she met anyone? Has she been to Brest?'

'No – Brest is rather far from where she is staying.'

The question seemed strange.

Misa was wearing a blue and green glass bracelet; I lifted her wrist to look at it more closely. She leaned towards me; I put my arm round her waist and she made no resistance. I felt her naked under the silk négligée. She looked at me anxiously, questioningly. I drew her to me, found her lips and felt the firmness of her breasts against my chest, as I had on the day we wrestled together. She let herself fall backwards and there on the cushions in front of the fire she became my mistress. I had no feeling of love, but desired her and reflected: 'if I don't take her now I shall look like a coward.'

We found ourselves seated opposite the dying embers of the last log. I held her hand; she was looking at me with a happy triumphant smile. I felt sad and would have liked to die.

'What are you thinking about?' said Misa.

'I'm thinking of poor Odile . . .'

She grew angry and two hard lines showed on her forehead as she said:

'Listen – I love you—I can't bear you to say such ridiculous things.'

'Why ridiculous?'

She hesitated and looked at me, thoughtfully.

'Don't you really understand – or are you pretending?'

I foresaw what she wanted to tell me. I ought to have stopped her, but wanted to know the worst.

'It is true,' I said, 'I don't understand.'

'Oh – I thought you understood but loved Odile too much to leave her or even to speak to her about it . . . I have often thought I ought to tell you everything. But I was Odile's friend; it was difficult for me . . . but now it does not matter. I care a thousand times more for you than I do for her.'

She told me that Odile had been François' mistress for six months and had begged her, Misa, to pass on their letters in case a Toulon postmark should attract my attention.

'You can understand how hard this was for me . . . all the more because of my love for you . . . Haven't you realised that I have been in love with you for three years? . . . Men understand nothing. But now at last everything is all right. You will see I shall know how to make you happy. You deserve it. I admire you so much . . . You have a wonderful character.'

She overwhelmed me with praise for several minutes. It gave me no pleasure and I only thought: 'How untrue all this is. I am not wonderful at all! I can't do without Odile . . . Why am I here? Why is my arm round this woman's waist? – for we were still seated side by side in the posture of happy lovers, and I hated her.

'Misa, how can you betray Odile's confidence? What you are doing is despicable.'

She looked at me in astonishment.

'Oh! That's the last straw . . . that you should defend her!'

'You are behaving very badly to Odile, even if it is for my sake. Odile is your friend . . .'

'She was; I don't like her any more.'

'Since when?'

'Since I began to love you.'

'I sincerely hope you don't love me . . . I adore Odile, whatever she is, and I find it very difficult to say why – perhaps it is because she never bores me, and she is my life and my joy.' I looked at Misa defiantly, she was trembling.

Misa said bitterly:

'You are extraordinary.'

'Perhaps!'

She hesitated a moment, then put her head on my shoulder and spoke in deeply passionate terms that might have touched me if I had not been so infatuated and so blind.

'Well – I love you and will make you happy in spite of yourself . . . I shall be faithful and devoted to you . . . Julien is at Gandumas; he leaves me in peace; you can come to see me there if you like as he spends two days every week at Guichardie . . . You have lost the habit of happiness, I shall bring it you back.'

'Thank you,' I said coldly, 'I am quite happy.'

This scene continued far into the night. We assumed the attitude and gestures of lovers, but I felt an increasing resentment against her, a perverse and incomprehensible rancour. Nevertheless we parted affectionately and with a kiss.

I swore to myself not to return and yet I often went to see her during Odile's absence. Misa had an incredible audacity and gave herself to me in her parents' drawing-room where a maid could have come in at any moment. I stayed till two or three in the morning, nearly always in silence.

'What are you thinking about?' she kept asking me. I was thinking how false she was to Odile, but answered:

'Of you.'

Now remembering everything calmly, I can see that Misa

was not at all a bad woman but at that time I felt and behaved harshly towards her.

XVI

At last Odile returned; I went to meet her at the station. I made up my mind to say nothing. I knew very well what course a conversation with her would take if I spoke frankly. I would begin by reproaching her, she would deny everything. I should repeat Misa's story; she would say Misa was lying and I would know that Misa had told the truth.

All that was useless. Walking up and down the platform in an atmosphere of coal-dust and oil, surrounded by strangers, I repeated to myself that I could only be happy when she was with me and as it was impossible for me to break up our marriage, it would be better to enjoy the pleasure of seeing her again and avoid upsetting her. At other moments I thought: How cowardly of me. It would only take a week's determination on my part to force her to change or to resign myself to living without her.

A porter hung up a placard: 'Express from Brest.' I stood still. If I had stayed at another hotel in Florence in May 1909 I should never have known of Odile Malet's existence. Yet I would have lived and been happy. Why not begin again from this very moment and pretend that she does not exist?

I saw the fire from an engine in the distance and the curve of a train winding towards us. Everything seemed unreal. I could no longer imagine Odile's face. I moved forward. Heads looked out of the windows, men jumped from the train before it stopped, moving crowds collected and porters wheeled trucks. Suddenly I saw Odile's silhouette. A few seconds later she was beside me with a porter carrying her grey bag. She looked well and gay. As we got into the car she said: 'Dickie, let's stop and buy some champagne and caviare and have a little supper like the day we returned from our honeymoon.'

This may seem very hypocritical but one must know Odile to judge her. She had no doubt enjoyed her few days with François and was prepared to be happy in the present moment and make it as pleasant for me as she could. Seeing that I was depressed, and did not smile she said despairingly:

'Why! what's the matter now, Dickie?'

My resolutions to keep silent with her were never reliable. I immediately broke out with all the thoughts I had meant to conceal.

'I hear that François is at Brest.'

'Who told you that?'

'Admiral Garnier.'

'Well supposing he is! What of it? And why should you mind?'

'I mind because he was quite near Morgat and it was easy for him to go and see you.'

'Yes, so easy, if you want to know that he did come and see me. What does it matter to you?'

'You didn't write and tell me.'

'Are you sure? I thought I did . . . In any case if I didn't it was because I thought it unimportant – and so it is.'

'I don't agree with you. I also heard that you have been carrying on a secret correspondence with him.'

This went home and Odile was beside herself; I had never seen her so excited.

'Who told you that?'

'Misa.'

'Misa! The wretch. She is a liar! Did she show you any letters?'

'No, but why should she invent it?'

'I'm sure I don't know . . . from jealousy.'

'That is unbelievable rubbish, Odile.'

We arrived home. Odile produced her charming and innocent smile for the servants, then went to her room, looked in the mirror to arrange her hair and, seeing me behind her with my eyes fixed on her reflection, smiled at me too.

'Poor Dickie! I can't leave you alone for a week without your getting ideas in your head about me . . . You are very ungrateful. I thought of you all the time and I will prove it to you. Pass my bag.'

She opened it, pulled out a little parcel and handed it to me. It contained two books – the *Reveries d'un Promeneur solitaire* and the *Chartreuse*, both in early editions.

'Oh, Odile . . . thank you – how extraordinary – where did you find them?'

'I hunted in the streets of Brest, I wanted to bring you back something nice.'

'So you did go to Brest?'

'Of course, it was quite near, there was a boat service. I have wanted to see Brest for ten years . . . Aren't you going to give me a kiss for my little present? I so hoped it would be a success . . . I took a lot of trouble, you know . . . They are very rare, Dickie; I spent all my small savings on them.'

I kissed her. My feelings towards her were so complex that I hardly understood them myself. I detested and adored her. I believed her to be both innocent and guilty. The violent scene I had begun was turning into a friendly and intimate conversation.

We talked all the evening of Misa's treachery just as if her revelations (which were undoubtedly true) did not concern Odile and me but a couple of friends whose happiness we wanted to protect.

'I do hope you won't see her again,' said Odile.

I promised not to.

I never knew what happened the next day between Odile and Misa. Did they settle it on the telephone? Did Odile go to see Misa? I knew how outspoken and brutal she could be. Her insolent courage, so foreign to my reserved nature, both shocked and charmed me. I never met Misa again, nor heard her spoken of. I retained a dream-like memory of our brief liaison.

XVII

When suspicion enters the mind it destroys love by a succession of shocks. Odile's return, her sweetness and tact, and my pleasure at seeing her again, served to delay the imminent catastrophe. But from that time, we both knew we were living in a mined zone and that an explosion might occur at any moment. I could no longer speak to Odile without a shade of bitterness, however slight, appearing in my words or in the tone of my voice. Every banal remark conveyed an unexpressed reproach. My optimistic outlook of the first months of our marriage was succeeded by extreme pessimism. The beauty of nature, revealed to me by Odile, now revived melancholy reflections. Even her beauty seemed no longer perfect and I began to detect signs of falseness in her features. Yet five minutes later I would rediscover her smooth brow, her innocent eyes and love her again.

At the beginning of August we went to Gandumas. The

solitude, remoteness and absence of letters and telephone calls reassured me and gave me a few weeks' respite.

Sunlit fields, shady slopes covered with fir trees, had a great effect on Odile. Nature gave her an almost sensual pleasure, which she unconsciously associated with her companion, even if that companion was myself. When solitude shared by two people is not prolonged to the point of satiety or boredom, it brings about a certain heightening of feeling and confidence that draws them closer together. I believed Odile felt at that moment as near to me as I did to her.

One evening we were alone on the terrace looking across a wide expanse of hills and woods, towards a heather covered moor on the opposite slope. The sun was setting, the scene was still and peaceful. Human affairs seemed little. Suddenly I said all kinds of humble and loving things to Odile, but strangely enough, they came from a man already resigned to losing her.

'What a beautiful life we might have had, Odile . . . I loved you so much . . . Do you remember Florence and the time when I couldn't stop looking at you for an instant? . . . I am still so near to being like that, darling . . .'

'I am glad to hear you say so . . . I too loved you dearly. Good Heavens! how I believed in you . . . I said to my mother: "I have found the man who will hold me – always." And then I was disappointed . . .'

'It was because I too misunderstood. Why didn't you explain?'

'You know quite well, Dickie . . . because it was impossible. You see, your great mistake is that you expect too much of women. They cannot live up to it . . . But I am glad to think you will miss me when I am no longer with you . . .'

She spoke these words in a painfully prophetic tone that made a deep impression on me.

'But you will always be with me.'

'You know I will not,' she said.

At that moment my parents arrived.

I sometimes led Odile to my observatory and we gazed together into the miniature torrent at the bottom of the wooded gorge. She loved this spot and spoke of her youth, of Florence and of our dreams beside the Thames. I clasped her in my arms and she did not protest. She seemed happy. Why not admit, I thought, that we constantly renew our lives, and each time it happens the previous life turns into a dream. Am I the same man who used to embrace Denise Aubry in this very place? Perhaps Odile has forgotten François since she has been here?

But while I tried to reconstruct my happiness at any cost, I knew it was unreal and that probably the reason for the dreamy, blissful expression on Odile's face, as she leaned on the wall, was the thought that François loved her.

There was one other person at Gandumas who understood very clearly what was happening to our marriage; it was my mother. I have told you that she never liked Odile but being kind, and seeing me so much in love, she did not wish to show her feelings towards my wife. The morning before our departure I met her in the kitchen garden and she asked me to go for a walk with her.

'Yes, I should enjoy going down to the valley; I have not been there with you since I was thirteen or fourteen.'

This recollection touched her and she became more confidential than usual. At first she spoke of my father's health; he had arterio-sclerosis and the doctor was worried. Looking down at the pebbles on the path she said:

'What is wrong between you and Misa?'

'Why do you ask me that?'

'Because you have not once seen her since you arrived . . . Last week I invited them to lunch and she refused; that has never happened before . . . there must be something the matter.'

'Yes – there is something, Mama, but I can't tell you what it is . . . Misa has behaved badly to Odile.'

My mother walked on in silence and then said in a low voice, as if unwillingly:

'Are you sure Odile has not behaved badly to Misa? I don't want to interfere between you and your wife, but for once I must tell you that everyone blames you, even your father. You are too weak with her. You know how I hate gossip; I should like to believe that all I hear is untrue, but if it is, you should insist on Odile living in such a way as to put an end to her being talked about.'

I listened to her as I slashed at the grass with my stick. I knew she was right and had restrained herself for a long time; no doubt Misa had talked to her and perhaps told her everything. My mother had become attached to Misa since she came to live at Gandumas and thought highly of her. Yes, no doubt, she knew the truth. But hearing this attack on Odile, although it was a just and guarded one, my reaction was that of the Knight Errant and I defended her strongly. I affirmed a confidence in Odile that I did not feel and attributed virtues to her which I denied when she was present. Love creates strange solidarities and that morning it seemed my duty to make common cause with Odile against the truth. I also wanted to persuade myself that she still loved me. I quoted to my mother all the signs which could show that Odile cared for me; the two books she had found with so much trouble at Brest, the affectionate tone of her letters, her attitude since we had been at Gandumas. I was so emphatic that I think I shook my mother's conviction, but alas, not my own, which was only too strong!

I did not speak to Odile of this conversation.

XVIII

On our return to Paris François' shadow again drifted across our lives, indefinite but always present. I wondered how he communicated with Odile since the breach with Misa. I noticed Odile had adopted the habit of rushing to the telephone as soon as she heard the bell, as if she feared I might intercept a message that should be concealed from me. She only read books about the sea and fell into a sort of dream when looking at the most ordinary engravings representing waves or ships.

One evening a telegram arrived for her. She opened it, said: 'It's nothing,' and tore it into tiny pieces.

'But how can it be nothing, Odile? What is it?'

'A dress that is not ready . . .'

Hearing from Admiral Garnier, whom I had questioned, that François was at Brest, I might have been satisfied, but was not.

Sometimes, under the influence of inspiring music at a concert or of a fine autumn day, we regained brief moments of tenderness.

'If you would only tell me the whole truth, darling, about the past . . . I would try to forget, and we would begin a new hopeful life and trust each other.'

She shook her head despairingly, without bitterness or

resentment. She no longer denied that there was a past. She admitted nothing, but her confession though silent was implicit.

'No, Dickie, I can't, it is useless. Everything is so confused now . . . I should not have the strength to unravel it. And then I shouldn't know how to explain why I said or did certain things . . . I don't know any more . . . No, there is nothing to be done . . . I give it up.'

These affectionate conversations nearly always ended in hostile interrogations. Something she said surprised me; the dangerous questions rose to my lips, I restrained myself for an instant, then came out with it. Odile always tried her best to carry off such scenes light-heartedly but when she saw I was serious, lost her temper.

'Oh no, no!' she said, 'An evening with you is torture. I would rather go away. If I stay here I shall go mad . . .'

Then the terror of losing her calmed me. I apologised, half-heartedly, and saw that each of these quarrels loosened the already fragile tie between us.

What was it that held her so long, since we had no children? A greater part was pity, I think, and even a little love, for sometimes sentiments overlap, neither being completely extinct, and in women particularly there is often a desire to retain everything. Moreover, Odile's religious beliefs, though rarely expressed and much weakened by François' influence, still existed and inspired her with a horror of divorce. Perhaps she was also attached, if not to me, at least to our life together by her childish love of material objects? She liked our house which she had furnished herself with so much taste. On a little table in her boudoir were her favourite books and the Venetian vase which always held a single, beautiful flower. When she took refuge in this sanctuary she felt protected from me and from her own fears. It was difficult for her to tear herself away from this background. If she went to live with François she would have to stay in Toulon or Brest for the greater part of the year and give up most of her friends. François would not suffice to fill her life any more than I had done. I realise now that what she needed was the movement around her provided by the interest of watching the lives of the various men with whom she came in contact. She did not understand this herself. She thought her suffering was caused by being separated from François and that she could find happiness with him. He had the prestige for her of a person whom she had not yet fathomed and who seemed rich in unknown possibilities. I had been this mythical and seductive person when we were in Florence and during our visit to England, but I had not been able to live up to the level of the fictitious image she had made of me. I was condemned. Now it was François' turn. He was going to be tested, would he survive it?

I believe if he had lived in Paris his liaison with Odile would have developed like similar maladies, and would have had no worse results than her discovering that she had overestimated him.

But he was far away and she could not do without him. What were his feelings? He must have been moved by the conquest of such a beautiful being, but if he were the kind of man I had been led to believe, marriage would not appeal to him.

I knew that François was passing through Paris about Christmas time on his way from Brest to Toulon. During the two days he was there Odile's behaviour was madly imprudent. She was informed of his arrival by a telephone call one morning, before I left for the office. I knew at once who it was by the expression of her face as she talked. I had never known her to look so tender, submissive and almost suppliant. She did not realise that although so far away from her lover, she was betraying herself by her ravishing and brilliant smile.

'Yes,' she said, 'I am glad to hear you . . . yes, yes . . . but . . .' She looked doubtfully at me, then said:

'Listen – call me again in half an hour.'

I asked her to whom she had been talking and she hung up the receiver indifferently without replying, as if she had not heard.

I managed to come back at lunch time and the maid then handed me a piece of paper on which Odile had written:

'If you come home, don't worry. I am obliged to go out for lunch. See you this evening, darling.'

'Has Madam been out long?' I asked.

'Yes – since ten o'clock.'

'With the car?'

'Yes, sir.'

I lunched alone and felt so miserable that I decided not to return to the office. I wanted to see Odile as soon as she came in and this time I was determined to ask her to choose between us.

I passed the afternoon in torture. About seven o'clock the telephone rang.

'Hallo' – said Odile's voice – 'Is that you, Juliette?'

'No – it is I, Philippe.'

'So you've come home? Well, I wanted to ask you if you'd mind if I dined here – '

'What! But where are you? And why? You have already lunched out.'

'Yes – but listen . . . I am at Compiègne at this moment

and as in any case I should be too late for dinner by the time I got home . . .'

'What are you doing at Compiègne at this hour?'

'I went for a walk in the forest; it was delightful in this dry cold weather. I didn't think you would be in for lunch.'

'Odile, I don't want to argue on the telephone, but all this is preposterous. Come home.'

She returned at ten o'clock and in answer to my reproaches said:

'Well – it will be the same tomorrow. I can't shut myself up in Paris in this weather.'

Once again she had the air of pitiless determination which had struck me when she took the train to Brest and had made me feel she would stop at nothing to attain her desire.

The next day it was she who asked me very sadly for a divorce and to allow her to live with her parents until she could marry François. We were in her boudoir before dinner. I made little resistance; I had known for a long time that our marriage must end like this and her attitude during François' stay in Paris had almost convinced me that it would be better to see her no more. Yet my first thought was an unworthy one; a Marcenat had never been divorced and it would be humiliating to tell my family about this drama. But I was so ashamed of the thought that I made it a point of honour to consider only Odile's interests.

Soon our conversation reached a high moral tone and as always happened when we were sincere with each other, we became affectionate. Dinner was announced and we went down. Seated opposite each other we hardly spoke, because of the servant. I looked at the plates and glasses, all these things showed Odile's taste; then I looked at her – perhaps it was the last time I should see that face which had brought me so much happiness. Pale and thoughtful her eyes gazed into mine, as if she also wanted to fix in her memory the features she would doubtless never see again.

After dinner we went to her boudoir and talked long and seriously of what our future would be. She gave me some advice:

'You must marry again. I am sure you would be a perfect husband for someone else. But I was not made for you . . . Only don't marry Misa, that would hurt me and she is a bad woman. I tell you who would suit you very well – your cousin Renée . . .'

'You are mad darling. I shall never marry again.'

'Oh, but you must . . . And then when you think of me do so without too much bitterness. I loved you very much, Dickie, and I know well what you are worth. If I have never told you how much I think of you it is because I am shy and it is not my way. But often I have seen you doing things that no other man would have done in your place and thought: "He is really a good man, all the same, Dickie . . ." And I even want to tell you something that may please you; in many ways I like you better than François, only . . .'

'Only?' I said.

'Only . . . he is indispensable to me. After I have spent a few hours with him I have the illusion of being strong, of living better and more fully. Perhaps it is not true; I should probably have been happier with you. But there it is – it didn't work. It is not your fault Philippe, it is no one's fault.'

When we separated very late at night she spontaneously offered me her lips.

'Oh,' she said, 'we are so unhappy.'

A few days later I received a kind and sad letter from her;

she said she had loved me for a long time and had never had a lover before François.

That is the story of my marriage. I don't know if I have been able to do justice as much as I wished to my poor Odile. I should have liked to make you feel her charm, her mysterious melancholy and her profound childishness.

She was of course judged severely by our friends and my parents. I who knew her as well as she could be known, think that no woman was ever less guilty.

XIX

After Odile left I was very unhappy. The house seemed so sad that I could hardly bear to stay in it. Sometimes in the evening I went into Odile's room, sat in a chair beside her bed as I used to, and thought about our lives. I was troubled by vague feelings of remorse; yet I had no definite reason for self-reproach. I had married Odile for love, though my family would have liked me to make a more brilliant match. I had been faithful to her until that evening with Misa and my brief betrayal was caused by Odile's. Certainly I had been jealous but she had done nothing to allay my fears. Nevertheless I felt responsible. I began to perceive a truth that was quite new to me about the relations that should exist between men and women. I saw women as unstable beings always in search of someone to guide them, to direct their minds and their errant desires. Perhaps a woman's need creates an obligation on the man's part to be the infallible compass, always pointing in the right direction. A great love is not sufficient to hold a woman unless the lover knows how to fill her life with renewed interests. What could Odile find in me? I came home every evening from the office where I had seen the same men, studied the same questions; I sat down in my armchair, looked at my wife and enjoyed her beauty. How could she find happiness in my invariable admiration? Women attach themselves naturally to men whose lives are full of activity, who give them an object to live for and make demands on them.

I looked at Odile's bed. What would I not give now to see her fair head on the pillow? How little I had given when there was still something to preserve. Instead of trying to understand her tastes I had condemned them and attempted to impose my own upon her.

The terrifying silence that enveloped me in that empty house was my punishment for an attitude which, though not unkind, was without nobility.

I ought to have left Paris but I could not make up my mind to go away; I found a mournful satisfaction in clinging to the smallest objects that reminded me of Odile. When half awake in the morning I seemed to hear a clear sweet voice calling through the open door: 'Good morning, Dickie!'

This January was like spring: the bare trees stood out against a cloudless blue sky. If Odile had been there she would have put on what she called 'a little tailored suit', wound her silver fox fur round her neck and would have been out since the morning.

'Alone?' I would have asked her in the evening. 'Oh,' she would have said, 'I don't remember . . .' and in face of this absurd mystery I should have felt an anguish that I now thought was unjustified.

I spent my nights trying to understand when the trouble

began. On our return from England we were perfectly happy. Perhaps if in one of our earlier discussions I had taken a stronger line and shown firmness and kindness, things would have been different. Our destiny is decided by a gesture, a word, the slightest effort at first might have sufficed to save the situation. Now I felt that the most heroic acts would not have revived the love Odile once had for me.

Before she went away we came to an understanding about our divorce proceedings. We agreed that I should write her an offensive letter which would cause the divorce to be pronounced against me. A few days later I was summoned to the Law Courts for the conciliation. It was painful to see Odile in such surroundings. Twenty couples were waiting, the men separated from the women by a grating, to avoid unpleasant scenes. People insulted each other from a distance, women cried. My neighbour, a chauffeur, said to me:

'It is some consolation that there are so many of us.'

Odile nodded to me and gave me a sweet affectionate glance and I knew I still loved her.

At last our turn came. The judge was a benevolent man with a grey beard. He told Odile not to be distressed; spoke of our mutual memories and the ties of marriage, then advised us to make a last attempt at reconciliation. I said:

'Unfortunately it is no longer possible.'

Odile stared fixedly in front of her. She looked as if she were suffering. 'Perhaps she is sorry,' I thought, 'perhaps she does not love him as much as I believed . . . perhaps she is already disappointed in him?'

Then as we both remained silent the judge said:

'In that case, kindly sign this affidavit.'

Odile and I went out together.

'Would you care to have a little stroll?' I said.

'Yes – it is such a lovely day. What a marvellous winter.'

I reminded her that she had left many of her belongings at home and asked if I should have them sent to her parents' house.

'Just as you like, but do keep whatever you want . . . I need nothing; and I shall not live very long, Dickie. You will soon be rid of my memory.'

'Why do you say that, Odile? Are you ill?'

'Oh no – not at all! It is an impression . . . mind you replace me quickly, if I were sure you were happy it would help me to be happy too.'

'I could never be happy without you.'

'Yes you will – you will soon see how relieved you will feel to be rid of an unbearable woman . . . I'm not joking, you know, it's true that I'm unbearable . . . How pretty the Seine is at this time of year.'

She stopped before a shop window where some naval charts were displayed; I knew she liked them and said:

'Shall I buy them for you?'

She looked at me sadly and tenderly.

'How good you are,' she said, 'Yes, I should like you to; it will be my last present from you.'

We went in to buy the two charts; then she called a taxi, took off her glove and gave me her hand to kiss, saying:

'Thank you for everything . . .'

She got in without looking back.

XX

In my great solitude my family was not much help. At heart my mother was glad that I was rid of Odile. She did not say so as she knew that I was suffering, but I felt it, therefore conversation was difficult between us. My father was very ill; he had had a cerebral congestion that left him with a paralysed hand and a slight distortion of the mouth, which spoilt his handsome face. He knew he could not recover and had become silent and grave.

I did not want to go back to Aunt Cora's as her dinners revived painful memories. The only person I could see who did not annoy and bore me was my cousin Renée. She was very tactful and did not mention my divorce. She was studying for a Science degree. I heard she did not want to marry. She was the first person I had met since my sorrow whose conversation interested me and distracted my thoughts from ceaseless brooding. She had devoted her life to research, a career which appeared to make her calm and contented. Was it possible to renounce love? I could not yet conceive any object in life other than devoting myself to an Odile but I found Renée's presence soothing. She came to lunch with me and I saw her often. After a few meetings I got accustomed to her and spoke openly about my wife and tried to explain what it was that I had loved so much in her. Renée asked me:

'When you are divorced, will you marry again?'

'Never,' I replied . . . 'And have you never thought of marrying?'

'No – I have a profession that fills my life and I am independent; I have never met a man who appealed to me.'

'What about all those doctors?'

'They are colleagues.'

Towards the end of February I went to spend a few days in the mountains and was recalled by telegram to say that my father was dying. My mother nursed him with admirable devotion; I watched her during the last night when he had already lost consciousness. Standing beside that inert body, wiping his forehead, moistening his lips, I marvelled at the serenity she retained in her great sorrow. I felt that it came from the knowledge of her virtuous life. My parents' lives seemed to me very beautiful, but impossible to understand. My mother had never wanted the pleasures that Odile and most young women I knew desired. While still young she had renounced all romantic ideas and thoughts of worldly pleasures; now she had her compensation. I sadly reviewed my own life; it would have been comforting to imagine Odile standing beside me at the end of this difficult journey, wiping the sweat of agony from my brow; a white haired Odile, softened by age, who had long since passed the stress of youthful emotions. Should I be alone one day in the face of death? I wished it might be as soon as possible.

I no longer had even indirect news of Odile. She believed that absolute silence would help me to forget her and warned me not to expect her to write. I heard she had rented a small villa near François' and no longer saw any of the friends we had in common.

As to myself I decided to leave our house, too big for me alone, and which recalled many unhappy memories. I found a nice apartment in an old house in the rue Duroc and took pains to furnish it in a way Odile would have liked. Who could tell? Perhaps one day she would come there, unhappy and wounded, and ask me for shelter. While turning out drawers I found a pile of letters written to Odile by her friends. I read them. Perhaps I was wrong but I could not resist the desire to know what they contained. As I have already told you, these letters were affectionate but innocent.

I spent the summer at Gandumas in almost complete solitude. I could only find a little peace lying in the fields far from the house. Then it seemed to me that all social links were broken and that I had regained for a moment contact with a deeper and truer reality for which I craved. Was a woman worth so much suffering? . . . Books only revived my sombre reflections because unfortunately I chose those that recalled my unhappy story.

In October I returned to Paris. A few young women came to see me, attracted as they always are by a solitary man. They merely passed through my life. To my surprise I resumed without effort the attitude of my youth. I behaved in the same way to women as I did before my marriage.

Nothing makes one more cynical than a great love that is unrequited; it also makes one more modest. I was surprised to find myself sought after. The truth is that when passion grips a man strongly, women are drawn to him against his wish. Obsessed by another, he becomes indifferent and almost brutal, even if he is by nature sentimental and loving. Being unhappy he allows himself to accept the affection that is offered him. He plays a dangerous game and conquers because he has been defeated. That was my case. I had never been more convinced of my inability to please, or desired less to do so and I had never received so many proofs of devotion and love. But it gave me no pleasure.

In my diary of 1913, interspersed with appointments, I find on every page references to Odile. I copy some for you at random:

October 20th. Her exactingness. How much one prefers people who are difficult to please. How pleasant it was to arrange for her with diffidence a bunch of wild flowers – cornflowers, marguerites, sunflowers – or a symphony in white arum lilies and white tulips . . .

Her humility. 'I know quite well what you want me to be like – very serious, very pure . . . a very good bourgeois French housewife . . . and yet be sensual, but only with you . . . you'd better give it up as hopeless, Dickie, I shall never be like that.'

Her modest pride. 'Yet I have quite a lot of small qualities . . . I have read more than most women . . . I know a lot of beautiful verses by heart . . . I can arrange flowers . . . I dress well . . . and I love you, yes, perhaps you don't believe it, but I love you very much.'

October 25th. There should exist a love so perfect that every feeling could be shared at the same instant with the beloved. There were some days, before I knew François well when I was almost grateful to him for being so nearly the man Odile could love . . . But then jealousy was stronger and François too imperfect.

October 28th. To love in others what little of you they contain.

October 29th. Sometimes you were impatient with me; I loved your impatience too!

A little further on I find this short note:

'I have lost more than I possessed.' It exactly expresses my feelings at that time. When Odile was present, much as I loved her I was alienated from her by her faults; when absent she became the goddess and by endowing her with the virtues she lacked I again became her Knight Errant. During our engagement my superficial knowledge of her produced the same distortion of love and desire, as distance and faithlessness were doing now. I loved Odile when distant and faithless more than I ever had when she was present and devoted.

XXI

Towards the end of the year I heard of Odile and François' marriage. It was a painful moment but the knowledge that henceforth there was nothing to be done helped me to find the courage to live.

After my father's death I made many changes in the management of the paper-works, had more leisure and was able to get in touch with some of the friends of my youth from whom my marriage had separated me, particularly André Halff and Bertrand. I tried to resume my neglected reading and studies and began to attend lectures at the Sorbonne and the College de France. It was surprising to find myself so changed and so indifferent to problems that formerly absorbed me. Had I really been so seriously concerned as to whether I was an idealist or a materialist? All metaphysics had ceased to interest me.

I left my office at five o'clock in the afternoon, went into society far more than in former days and noticed with sadness that I now sought the pleasures Odile had tried so hard to force upon me.

Many women I had met at Avenue Marceau, knowing me to be alone and fairly free, invited me to their houses. On Saturday evenings I went to Hélène de Thianges who was always at home on that day. She received men of letters, politicians and important business men. Her father, M Pascal-Bouchet, was an industrialist and occasionally arrived from Normandy with his second daughter Françoise.

Though suffering still acutely from my wound, I could now pass whole days without thinking of Odile or François. As Odile was now Mme de Crozant many people did not know she had been my wife and having met her in Toulon, where she was considered the beauty of the town, they sometimes spoke of her in my presence. Hélène de Thianges tried to silence them or to lead me away but I wanted to listen. It was not generally thought that the marriage was going well. Yvonne Prévost was often in Toulon and I asked her to tell me frankly what she knew.

'It is very difficult to explain; I have not seen much of them . . . My impression is that even on the day of their marriage they both already knew they were making a mistake. And yet she loves him . . . Forgive me for telling you this Marcenat, but you asked me. She certainly loves him more than he loves her, but she tries to hide it because of her pride. I had a meal with them . . . The atmosphere was distressing . . . She said some of those nice, rather naïve little things that you used to admire and François snubbed her . . . He is so brutal at times, it hurts me . . . one could see she was trying to please him and wanted at all costs to talk of subjects that would interest him . . . of course she did not talk about them well, and François replied in an impatient, contemptuous manner – "Oh yes, Odile – of course, yes." Roger and I felt sorry for her.'

I spent the winter of 1913-14 in trivial intrigues with women, unnecessary business trips and studies that were never fruitful as I was unable to take anything seriously.

Towards the end of May Hélène de Thianges began to give garden parties. She threw cushions on the lawn for the women and the men sat on the grass. The first Saturday in June there was a gathering of writers and politicians grouped round l'abbé Cenival. Hélène's little dog was at her feet and she said very seriously:

'Father, have animals got souls? Because if they haven't I

just don't understand anything. How can my little dog who has suffered so much . . .'

'But of course,' he answered, 'why should you think they haven't? . . . They have very small souls.'

'It is not very orthodox,' said someone, 'but it is disturbing.'

I was sitting a little way off with an American, Beatrice Howell, listening to the conversation.

'I am sure they have souls,' she said, 'there is really no difference between them and us . . . I was thinking of this only today when I spent the afternoon at the Zoo. I adore animals, Marcenat.'

'So do I – shall we go there together one day?'

'With pleasure . . . what was I saying? Oh yes – this afternoon I was watching the otters. I like them because they shine like wet rubber. They were turning round in circles under the water, raising their heads every two minutes to breathe, and I felt sorry for them, thinking what a monotonous life the poor beasts had. Then I thought: "And how about us? What are we doing but turning round in circles under water all the week and on Saturdays at six o'clock we show our heads at Hélène's, on Tuesdays at the Duchess of Rohan's, or Madelaine Lemaire's and on Sundays at Mme de Martel's . . ." It is much the same thing don't you think?'

At this moment I saw Commander Prévost and his wife arriving; I was struck by their grave expression. Hélène rose to greet them. I watched her because I liked the gracious animation she showed when welcoming her guests. I always told her she looked like a white butterfly alighting delicately here and there.

The Prévosts began telling her something and her face became serious. She looked round uneasily, and seeing me turned her eyes away. They moved a few steps further off.

'Do you know the Prévosts?' I asked Beatrice Howell.

'Yes – I have been to their house in Toulon. They have a lovely old place . . . I like those quays at Toulon, the sea and the old French houses blend so beautifully.'

Several people had now joined Hélène and the Prévosts. They were all talking rather loudly and I thought I heard my name.

'What is the matter?' I said to Mrs Howell. 'Let's go and see.'

I helped her to get up and brushed a few blades of grass from her dress.

Hélène saw us coming and moved towards me.

'Excuse me,' she said to Beatrice, 'I would like a word with Marcenat.'

'Listen,' she said, 'I am heart-broken to be the first to tell you this appalling news, but I don't want to risk – well – the Prévosts have just told me that your wife . . . that Odile killed herself this morning at Toulon, with a revolver.'

'Odile? – My God! Why?'

I imagined Odile's frail body pierced by a bleeding wound and a phrase went through my head: 'Under the influence of Mars, fatally condemned . . .'

'Nobody knows,' she said. 'Leave at once without saying goodbye to anyone. As soon as I know anything I will telephone.'

I started walking at random towards the Bois. What could have happened? My poor child, why hadn't she sent for me if she was unhappy? With what wild joy I would have gone to her rescue and taken her back and consoled her! From the first day I had seen François I knew he would be Odile's evil genius. I recalled that dinner party and the vivid impression I had of being a father who has unwittingly brought his child into a contaminated area. That day I felt she must be saved as soon as possible. I had not saved her . . .

Odile dead . . . Passing women looked at me anxiously. Perhaps I was talking out loud . . . So much beauty, so much charm . . . I remembered standing by her bed, holding her hand while she recited to me:

> From too much love of living
> From hope and fear set free . . .

'*The weariest river*, Dickie,' she said to me in an assumed doleful voice . . . And I replied: 'Don't talk like that, darling, you will make me cry.'

Odile dead . . . Ever since we met I had looked at her with a superstitious fear. Too beautiful . . . One day at Bagatelle an old gardener said to us:

'The most beautiful roses fade the soonest . . .'

Odile dead . . . If I had been able to see her again for a quarter of an hour with the understanding that I should then die with her, I would have accepted at once.

I don't know how I got home or went to bed. Towards daybreak I fell asleep and dreamt I was dining with Aunt Cora. The other guests were André Halff, Hélène de Thianges, Bertrand and my cousin Renée. I looked everywhere for Odile. At last, after prolonged anxiety, I found her stretched out on a sofa. She was pale and seemed very ill and I thought: 'Yes – she is ill, but she is not dead. What a ghastly dream!'

XXII

My first impulse was to go to Toulon the next day, but for a week I was feverish and delirious. Bertrand and André nursed me with great devotion; Hélène brought me flowers several times. When I recovered my balance I asked her anxiously what she knew. The accounts she had heard, like those I was given later myself, were contradictory.

The truth seemed to be that François, accustomed to complete independence, had soon tired of the marriage. Odile had disappointed him. Indulged by me, she had shown herself to be rather exacting just at the time when François loved her less. He had thought her intelligent; she was not, at least not in the ordinary sense of the word. I knew this well, but did not mind. He had tried to impose a discipline on her mind and on her behaviour. They were both proud and had offended each other deeply.

Sometime later a woman told me what François had confided to her about Odile.

'She was very beautiful,' he said, 'and I really loved her. But her first husband had spoilt her. She was madly coquettish. She was the only woman who ever made me suffer . . . I defended myself . . . I dissected her and showed her up naked and exposed. I saw all the workings of her small, deceitful mind . . . and showed her that I saw them . . . She thought she could recapture me by exercising her charm . . . Then she understood that she was defeated . . . Naturally I regret what has happened, but I have no remorse. There is nothing I can do now.'

When I knew about this conversation I had a horror of François. Yet at times I admired him. He had been stronger than I was and possibly more intelligent; above all stronger. I understood Odile just as he had done but the difference between us was that I had not the courage to tell her so. Was François' cynicism more admirable than my weakness? After long and serious reflection I too regretted nothing. To destroy a woman and bring her to despair is easy. I still think, even after my failure, that it was finer to try to love her, even against her will.

All that, however, does not clearly explain Odile's suicide. What is certain is that François was not in Toulon on the day she killed herself. During the war Bertrand met a young man who had dined with Odile on the eve of her suicide. There were three naval officers and three other women friends present. The conversation had been very gay. While drinking champagne Odile had laughingly said to her companions:

'You know, I shall kill myself tomorrow at midday.'

She had been calm all the evening and this unknown man had noticed and described to Bertrand the white, luminous brilliance of her beauty.

I was ill for a month. Then I went to Toulon. I spent several days there, covering Odile's grave with white flowers. One evening at the cemetery an old woman came up to me and said she had been Mme de Crozant's maid and recognised me from the photograph in one of her mistress's drawers. She went on to say that in the first weeks Odile, while appearing very gay in public, looked in despair as soon as she was alone.

'Sometimes, when I went in to Madam's room I found her sitting in an armchair, her head on her hands . . . she seemed as if she were looking at death.'

I talked to her for a long time and was glad to see that she had adored Odile.

There was nothing for me to do in Toulon and at the beginning of July I decided to go and live at Gandumas. There I tried to work and read, went for long walks over the moors and got sleep through air and exercise. I continued to dream of Odile nearly every night, and usually saw myself in a church or a theatre; the place next to me was empty. Suddenly I thought: 'Where is Odile?' I searched for her and saw pale, dishevelled women but none of them looked like her. Then I woke up.

It was impossible for me to work or even go to the factory. I had no wish to see any human being and clung to my sorrow. Each morning I went alone towards the village; the sound of the organ coming from the church was so delicate and fluid that it mingled with the air and seemed to be part of it. I imagined Odile beside me in the light dress she wore the day we walked together for the first time in Florence under the black cypresses. Why was she lost to me? I sought the word or act that had transformed this great love into such a sad story, but I could not find it. In all the gardens there were roses that she would have loved. It was during one of these walks to Chardeuil on a Saturday in August that I heard the rolling of drums and a voice calling out: 'Mobilisation of armed forces by land and sea.'

PART TWO

ISABELLE

ISABELLE

I

PHILIPPE, I have come to work in your study and it is hard to believe that I shall not find you here. You are still so living to me. I see you sitting in your armchair, a book in your hand, then at your table, your eyes evading mine as you no longer listen to my words. I see you receiving a friend and endlessly turning a pencil round between your long fingers. It is three months since that agonising night when you said: 'Isabelle, I am suffocating. I believe I am going to die,' in a voice that was no longer yours. Shall I forget it? How terrible to think that my suffering may come to an end. I remember how it pained me when you said with your cruel sincerity: 'Now I have lost Odile for ever, I can no longer see her features.' You loved her deeply. I have just re-read the long story you wrote for me at the time of our marriage; through that, something of Odile will remain; of me, nothing. I envied her. Yet you loved me too, I have your letters of 1919. You loved me then, perhaps too much! I remember saying you overestimated me, that when you saw your mistake you would do me less than justice and think nothing of me. You told me that Odile once remarked: 'You expect too much of women and place them too high. It is dangerous.' She was right.

During the last fortnight I have resisted the desire which

grows ever stronger to write about our life for myself as you wrote about yours for me. Do you think I could do it, even badly? I want to write as you did, with truth and justice. It will be hard. One is tempted to be indulgent to oneself. It was one of my faults and you sometimes blamed me for it. You used to say: 'Don't pity yourself.' I have your letters and the red notebook you hid with such care. I have the little journal I began and you asked me to give up . . . I am sitting in your place. A frightening silence encloses me. Do I dare to try? . . .

II

Our house was in the rue Ampère. My white bedroom was gradually getting faded and dirty. My study was used as a store-room. I had my supper there with my governess when there were large dinner parties. The over-worked butler brought our meals consisting of lukewarm soup and melting ices at about ten o'clock. He seemed to understand as I did the obscure, almost humiliating, part I played as an only child in the house. How unhappy I was! You used to say: 'You were not as unhappy as you think you were.' No, I do not deceive myself. I was unhappy. Was it my parents' fault? I have often blamed them, but now softened by this more potent suffering, I look at the past with fresh eyes. I realise that they meant well but it seems to me their method was severe and dangerous as the result has shown.

I say 'my parents', I should say 'my mother', as my father who was always very busy only asked that his daughter should be silent and invisible. For a long time his aloofness gave him prestige in my eyes. I considered him a natural ally against my mother because several times he answered her in a tone of amused scepticism when she complained of my bad character.

'You remind me of my chief, M Delcassé; he places himself behind Europe and says he is making her advance . . . You think that one can mould another human being . . . oh no, my dear, we think we are actors but we are no more than spectators.'

My mother glanced at him reproachfully, anxiously drawing his attention to my presence by a gesture. She was not unkind but sacrificed my happiness and her own to imaginary dangers.

Later Philippe said to me: 'Your mother suffers from excessive prudence.' It was true. She regarded life as a hard fight, against which one must be inured.

'A spoilt girl will be an unhappy woman,' she used to say, 'one must not accustom a child to think she is well-off; God knows what is in store for her. It is bad for a girl to be paid compliments.' She repeatedly told me that I was not pretty and would find it difficult to make myself popular. She saw that this made me cry but in her view childhood was what earthly life is to those who fear hell; it was necessary, even at the price of harsh treatment, to guide my body and soul towards a temporal salvation, the entrance to which was marriage, the Last Judgement.

Perhaps such an education might have been good for me if I had had, like her, self-confidence, beauty and a strong will. But being shy by nature it made me sullen. From the age of eleven I avoided the company of others and sought refuge in reading. I had a passion for history, and the sufferings of the Carmelite and the martyrdom of Joan of Arc gave me a strange pleasure. I believed that I too would have been capable of unlimited physical courage. My father despised cowardice and forced me while still quite small to stay alone in the garden at night. When I was ill he wanted me to be treated without sympathy or tenderness. I trained myself to think of visits to the dentist as stages on the road towards heroic saintliness.

When my father left the Quai d'Orsay and was appointed Ambassador to Belgrade, my mother closed the house in the rue Ampère for several months of the year and sent me to stay with my grandparents at Lozère. There I was even more unhappy. I did not like the country. I preferred monuments to landscapes, and churches to forests. When I read over my diary of that period I have the impression of flying over a desert of boredom in a very slow aeroplane. It seemed as though I should never stop being fifteen, sixteen, seventeen years old. My parents, who believed they were bringing me up well, killed in me all taste for happiness. The first ball, which for many women has gay and brilliant memories, is associated in my mind with feelings of painful humiliation. It was in 1913. My mother had my dress made at home by her maid. I knew it was ugly but she despised luxury and said: 'Men do not look at dresses, one does not like a woman for her clothes.' I had no success at parties, I was awkward and was considered stiff, clumsy and pretentious. I was stiff because I spent my life in a state of repression, clumsy because I was allowed no freedom of movement or speech, pretentious because being too shy and modest to talk with ease of myself or of light and amusing matters, I took refuge in serious subjects. At dances my rather pedantic seriousness kept young men at a distance.

How I longed for the man who would remove me from this slavery, those long walks at Lozère when I saw no one, and knew in the morning that nothing would happen all day except an hour's walk with Mlle Chauvière. I imagined my deliverer, handsome and charming. Every time they gave *Siegfried* at the Opera I begged Mlle Chauvière to arrange for me to go, because I saw myself as a captive Walkyrie who could only be saved by a hero.

My repressed enthusiasm which took a religious form at the time of my first communion, found a new outlet during the war. In August 1914, having a nursing diploma, I asked to be sent to a hospital in the military zone. My father was then 'en poste' far from France and my mother with him. My grandparents, distracted by the declaration of war, allowed me to go. The ambulance I joined at Belmont had been presented by the Baronne Choin. The sister in charge of the hospital was Mlle Renée Marcenat. She was a beautiful proud and intelligent girl and saw at once that there were reserves of strength in me, and in spite of my youth made me her assistant.

I discovered there that people liked me. One day I heard Renée Marcenat say to Mme Choin: 'Isabelle is my best nurse; she has only one fault – she is too pretty.' This gave me great pleasure.

A second-lieutenant in the Infantry whom we nursed for a slight wound asked permission to write to me when he left the hospital. The thought of the dangers he would be exposed to prompted me to answer in a more emotional tone than I felt; he replied affectionately and from one letter to another I found myself engaged to him. I could not believe it. It seemed to me unreal but at that time life was mad and everything was done at top speed. When my parents were consulted they wrote that Jean de Cheverny belonged to a good family and they approved of my marriage. I knew nothing about Jean. He was gay and handsome. We had four days of solitude in an hotel in the Place de l'Etoile, then he rejoined his regiment and I went back to the hospital. That was the whole of my married life. Jean had counted on getting another leave during the winter, but was killed at Verdun in February 1916. At that moment I thought I loved him. When I received his papers and a little photograph of myself found on him after his death I cried a great deal and in good faith.

III

My father was appointed Minister to Pekin at the time of the Armistice. He asked me to accompany him there; I refused. I was too accustomed to independence to tolerate family control again. My income enabled me to live alone. With my parents' approval I converted the second floor of their house into a small flat and linked my life with Renée Marcenat's. After the war she entered the Pasteur Institute where she distinguished herself. She had no difficulty in employing me to work with her in the laboratory.

I became attached to Renée and admired her. I envied the authority with which she acted, yet I felt that she was vulnerable. She tried to give the impression that she did not wish to marry, but by the tone of her voice when talking of her cousin Philippe Marcenat, I felt she was in love with him.

'He is a very reserved person,' she said, 'and seems aloof if one does not know him well, but in reality he is almost frighteningly sensitive . . . The war did him good by forcing him away from his normal life. He is no more fit to be the director of a paper-works than I am to be a great actress . . .'

'But why? Does he do anything else?'

'No, he reads a lot and is very cultivated . . . he is a most remarkable person, I assure you . . . you would like him immensely.'

Many young men now paid me attention. Post-war standards were free and easy and I was alone. In the circle of doctors and young scholars who surrounded Renée I met interesting men but there was no-one who really attracted me. I could not believe it when they said they loved me. My mother's verdict: 'You are unfortunately plain', obsessed me, in spite of the denials I heard when I was a nurse. A sense of inferiority was deeply implanted in me. I thought men either wanted to marry me for my money or take me as an easy and unexacting mistress for a few evenings.

Renée brought me an invitation to dine with the Baronne Choin; she herself went quite often on Tuesdays.

'It would bore me,' I said, 'I hate society.'

'No, you will see she nearly always has interesting people. And next Tuesday my cousin Philippe will be there and if you are bored we can always make a little group of three.'

'Oh, very well – I should like to meet him.'

Renée succeeded in making me want to know Philippe Marcenat. When she told me the story of his marriage I remembered having met his wife and thinking her very beautiful. It was said that he still loved her and although Renée evidently did not approve of all her actions, she admitted that it was impossible to find a more perfect face.

'Only,' she said, 'I cannot forgive her for the way she behaved to Philippe who was loyalty itself to her.'

I asked many details about the marriage and even read certain passages in Philippe's letters to Renée during the war and liked their melancholy tone.

Mme Choin's broad staircase and her numerous flunkeys

displeased me. Entering the drawing-room I saw Renée standing near the mantelpiece beside a very tall man with his hands in his pockets. Philippe Marcenat was not handsome but I thought he looked kind and reassuring. When he was introduced to me it was the first time in my life that I did not feel shy with a stranger. I was pleased to find myself placed next to him at table. After dinner an instinctive manoeuvre brought us together.

'Would you like to have a quiet talk?' he asked, 'if so come with me, I know this house very well.'

He took me into the Chinese boudoir. What I remembered of this conversation was an exchange of the experiences of our childhood. Philippe told me about his life at Limousin and we were amused to find how similar our youth and our families had been. Gandumas was furnished like our house in the rue Ampère. Philippe's mother, like mine, had said: 'Men do not notice clothes.'

'Yes, this peasant and bourgeois heredity of so many French families is very strong and in a certain way rather fine,' he said, 'but for me it is no longer any good, I have lost my faith . . .'

'Not I,' I replied laughingly, 'do you know there are things that I just can't do . . . although I live alone, I could not buy flowers or sweets for myself. It would seem to me immoral and would give me no pleasure.'

He looked at me in astonishment.

'Do you really mean that? You can't buy flowers?'

'I can for a dinner or a tea party, but just for myself, for the mere pleasure of looking at them – no I can't.'

'Don't you like them?'

'Oh yes . . . but I can quite well do without them.'

I thought I saw a sad, ironic look in his eyes and changed

the subject. No doubt it was this second part of our conversation that struck Philippe because in his red diary I find this note:

March 23rd, 1919. Dined at Aunt Cora's. Spent all the evening with Renée's pretty friend, Mme de Cheverny, in the Chinese boudoir. Strange . . . She is not at all like Odile and yet . . . Perhaps it was just because she was wearing a white dress . . . Gentle, shy . . . It was difficult to make her talk. Then she became confiding: 'Something happened this morning,' she said, 'which . . . I don't know how to tell you . . . well it made me indignant. A woman I hardly know, not an intimate friend, you understand, rang me up and said: "I'm pretending I am lunching with you today, Isabelle, don't give me away." How can one lie like that and expect to find an accomplice? I think it is a mean trick.'

'One must be indulgent; many women have difficult lives.'

'They have difficult lives because they make them so. They think that unless they surround themselves with an atmosphere of mystery they will be bored . . . It is not true; life is not made up of petty little intrigues. Don't you agree?'

Renée came and sat beside us saying: 'May I disturb this tête-a-tête?'

Then, as we were silent, she rose, laughing, and went away. Her friend remained pensive for a moment, then continued:

'Well, don't you think that love is only worth having if there is complete confidence between two people and they can look into each others minds and hearts without seeing a flaw?'

At this moment she no doubt thought she had hurt me and she blushed. It was true that her remark had wounded me a little. She then said a few kind words with an awkwardness that was touching. Renée returned with Dr Maurice de Fleury and there followed a conversation about the secretions of the endocrine glands. I admired Renée's precise mind. I received a pleasant farewell glance from her friend.

I also remember the phrase that had wounded Philippe and

thought about it when I got home. The next morning I wrote a few lines to tell him I was sorry to have been so clumsy in expressing my sympathy because, through hearing about him from Renée I had felt very friendly towards him for a long time. I added that I should be very glad, as he was alone, if he would come and see me sometimes. He replied:

> Your letter confirmed the impression I had formed from your face. You spoke of my sadness and loneliness with such natural, spontaneous sympathy and kindness, that I felt immediate confidence in you and gratefully accept the friendship you offer. You can have no idea how precious it will be to me.

I invited Philippe and Renée to lunch. Then we both lunched with him. I much admired his little flat and remember particularly two fine Sisleys (lavender-blue landscapes of the Seine) and the soft-coloured flowers on the table. Conversation was easy, amusing and serious at the same time and it was evident that we three got on well together.

It was then Renée's turn to invite Philippe and me and he offered to take us to the theatre the next day; we soon got in the habit of going out with him two or three times a week. During these outings I was amused to notice that Renée took care to make it evident that she and Philippe were the hosts and I was the guest. I accepted this attitude, but knew instinctively that Philippe would have preferred to be alone with me. One evening Renée was not well enough to come and he and I went out together. At dinner he spoke of his own accord and very frankly about his marriage. Then I understood that what Renée had told me about Odile was not altogether true. From her account I imagined Odile to be a very beautiful but dangerous woman. When listening to Philippe I saw her as a frail child who had tried her best. I very much liked him that evening and admired the tender memory he kept of a woman who had made him suffer. For the first time I began to think that perhaps he was the hero I was waiting for.

At the end of April he went for a long journey. He had not been well, coughed a good deal and his doctors advised a warm climate. I received a card from Rome:

Cara signora, I write to you in front of an open window; the sky is blue and cloudless; on the Forum the columns and triumphal arches emerge from a sandy golden haze. Everything is incredibly beautiful.

Then a card from Tangiers:

First stage of a dream journey on a sea of pearl grey and violet. Tangiers? It is reminiscent of Constantinople, Asnières and Toulon. It is dirty and grandiose like all the East.

Then a telegram from Oran:

Come to lunch with me Thursday one o'clock – kindest regards Marcenat.

That morning when I saw Renée at the laboratory, I said:

'So we're lunching with Philippe on Thursday?'

'What? Has he come back?'

I showed her the telegram: her face assumed a pained expression that I had never seen on it before. She quickly pulled herself together.

'Oh – I see,' she said, 'well you will lunch by yourselves as he has not invited me.'

I was very embarrassed. Later on I knew from Philippe himself that his principal reason for going away was to put an end to the intimacy between him and Renée. Their families treated them like an engaged couple, and this exasperated him. Renée slipped out of his life without a murmur. She remained our friend, though at times a rather embittered one. It was entirely through her that I had learned to admire Philippe, and yet from that moment Renée welcomed almost cruelly anything that placed him in a bad light.

Philippe said: 'It is only human,' but I was less indulgent.

IV

Throughout the summer Philippe and I saw a great deal of each other. He went to his office, took a few hours off each day, and only went to Gandumas once a month. He telephoned me every morning and in the afternoon when it was fine we took a walk, in the evening we went out to dinner or a theatre. Philippe was a most delightful friend and tried to gratify my slightest wish. He sent me flowers, a book we had talked about or something he admired during one of our walks. I say *he* admired because Philippe's tastes were quite different to mine. Here was a mystery that I tried in vain to solve. When we were together at a restaurant and women came in he expressed his opinion of their dresses, the particular degree of their elegance and commented on the character that these details seemed to reveal. I noticed with a kind of panic that his impressions were nearly always the opposite to mine. In my usual methodical way I tried to find rules for thinking in the Philippe manner and for seeing everything through his eyes. I failed.

'But surely that dress is pretty, isn't it?' I said.

'What!' he replied in disgust, 'that salmon-pink thing? Good heavens no!'

I admitted he was right but did not understand why.

When it was a question of books or theatres it was much the same. From our first conversations I noticed that he appeared shocked because I sincerely upheld Bataille as a great dramatic author or Rostand as a great poet.

'Well – yes,' he said, 'I was much amused, even enthusiastic about *Cyrano* when I was young and indeed it is very well done, but it is not on a high level.'

I thought him unjust but did not dare to defend my opinions as I was afraid of his disapproval. The books he gave me (Stendhal, Proust, Mérimée) bored me at first but I very soon got to like them because I saw why they pleased him. Nothing was easier to understand than Philippe's taste in books; he was one of those readers who seek only themselves in what they read. Often I found his books covered with marginal notes that I deciphered with difficulty and which helped me to follow his thoughts through those of the author. I was passionately interested in everything that revealed his character.

What astonished me most was that he took as much trouble to form my taste as to entertain me. No doubt I had many faults, but no vanity; I considered myself stupid and not very pretty and never stopped wondering what he could see in me. It was clear that he liked my company and wanted to please me. It was not that I had ever tried to attract him. My respect for Renée's prior rights prevented that from the beginning, so there was no doubt it was he who had chosen me. Why? I had the flattering but disquieting feeling that he gave me credit for having a richer and nobler soul than I really possessed. In the note which I have already quoted he wrote: 'She is not at all like Odile and yet . . . perhaps it is just because she was wearing a white dress . . .' I certainly did not resemble Odile in any way, but one can be subject to mysterious imaginary impressions that may profoundly influence one's life.

It is a mistake to say that love is blind; the truth is a lover is indifferent to faults and weaknesses that he sees quite clearly, if he believes he can find in the beloved some quality important to him, though perhaps indefinable. In his heart, and without admitting it to himself, Philippe knew that I was a gentle, shy and not a remarkable woman, but he needed my presence. He expected me to be ready to give up everything to be with him. I was not his wife or his mistress and yet he seemed to exact a scrupulous fidelity. Several times I went out with other friends as I had been accustomed to since the war. When I told him I saw that it made him so unhappy that I gave it up. He now rang me up every morning at nine o'clock. If I had already left for the Pasteur Institute, or if there was a delay in getting through for some other reason, I found him so agitated by the evening that I finally left the laboratory altogether so that he should always be able to find me. Thus little by little he took possession of my life.

He got into the habit of coming to see me after lunch at the rue Ampère. I knew Paris well and liked showing him old houses, churches and museums. He made fun of my precision and said laughingly:

'You know the dates of all the kings of France and the telephone numbers of all the great writers.'

But he enjoyed these walks. I knew now what he liked; for instance a splash of brilliant coloured flowers on a grey wall, a corner of the Seine glimpsed through a window from the Isle of Saint-Louis, a garden hidden behind a church. In the morning I often went alone to explore the ground so as to be sure of taking him in the afternoon to a place he would like. Sometimes we went to a concert; in music our tastes were nearly the same. This struck me because mine had not been formed by education but by spontaneous emotions I had experienced.

Thus we lived an intimate, almost conjugal life but Philippe did not say he loved me and even repeated that he did *not* love me which he thought was all the better for our friendship. One day, meeting me by chance in the Bois where we had each gone for a morning walk, he said:

'It is such a joy to see you that it seems as if I were recapturing the emotions of adolescence. When I was sixteen I used to try and meet a young woman called Denise Aubry in the streets of Limoges.'

'Did you love her?'

'Yes – and I got tired of her as you would get tired of me if I did not ration my happiness for myself.'

'But don't you believe in love being shared?'

'Even if it is shared, love is terrible. A woman once quoted a phrase which I think very true: "A love affair that goes well – that's to say so-so – is difficult, but a love that goes badly is hell".'

I did not answer; I had decided to let myself be led by him and to do whatever he wished . . . A few days later we went to the opera to see my dear *Siegfried*. It was a great pleasure to hear it sitting beside the man who had become my hero. During the 'Forest Murmurs' I placed my hand without thinking on Philippe's and he turned towards me with a questioning, happy look on his face. Coming back in the car he in turn took one of my hands, raised it to his lips and kept hold of it. When the car stopped in front of the door he said: 'Goodnight, darling.'

I replied with a rather excitable gaiety: 'Goodnight, my dear friend.'

The next morning I received a letter which he wrote

during the night: 'Isabelle, the unique and exacting sentiment I have for you is not only friendship . . .'

He described some romantic phases of his childhood; he spoke to me of the woman he had called 'The Queen' and then 'The Amazon' who had always obsessed him:

The type of woman who appealed to me was always the same. She had to be fragile, unhappy, also frivolous and yet wise. You see the robust authority of a Renée could have nothing in common with her. The moment I met Odile I knew she was the one I had always waited for. What can I say to you? You certainly have a little of that mysterious essence which for me holds the greatest compensation in life. It includes 'la douceur de vivre'; without it I have wished to die. Love, friendship? What does it matter what we call it? It is a deep, tender sentiment, a great hope. My darling, I long for your lips, and I want to touch the bristles at the back of your neck where your hair has been clipped. PHILIPPE

That evening I went out with him. We met at the Salle Gaveau to hear some Russian music. On arriving I said with a smile: 'Good evening . . . I got your letter.'

He became rather cold, and talked of something else. But in the car coming home I gave him the lips he had wanted for so long.

The following Sunday we went to the forest of Fontainebleau.

'I should love to show you, who are such a keen Wagnerian, a place near Barbizon that really reminds me of the ascent to Valhalla. It consists of boulders embedded under pine trees that rise towards the sky. It is chaotic and gigantic, yet very well organised, in fact altogether "The Twilight of the Gods". I know that you don't care for landscapes but you ought to like this one because it is rather theatrical.'

I had put on a simple white dress so as to be like a Walkyrie myself. Philippe admired it. In spite of my efforts it was seldom he liked my dresses; he nearly always studied them with a critical air and said nothing. That day I saw that he looked at me with pleasure. The forest was as beautiful as he had described it. A path wound through the huge moss-covered rocks. Several times Philippe held my hand to guide me over the stones and his arm closed round me when I had to jump. We stretched ourselves out on the grass, my head resting on his shoulder. Pine trees planted in a circle gave us the impression of being at the bottom of a dark well whose edges enclosed the blue sky.

V

I wondered if Philippe wanted to be my husband or my lover. My devotion to him was great enough to make me accept even this uncertainty. He should be the arbiter of my destiny and the decision must rest with him. I waited with confidence.

Sometimes a more definite indication seemed to be suggested by his words.

'I must show you Bruges,' he said, 'it is a delightful place . . . and we have not yet taken even the smallest trip together.'

The idea of going away with him enchanted me; I smiled affectionately but he did not refer to it again during the following days.

July was intensely hot. All our friends were going off for their holidays; I did not want to leave Paris as it would mean being separated from Philippe. One evening he took me to dine at Saint Germain. We stayed for a long time on the terrace. Paris was spread out at our feet, its twinkling lights resembled stars reflected in a dark sea. Couples were laughing in the shadows, voices singing in the arbours. Nearby a cricket in the grass serenaded us. While driving back in the car Philippe spoke of his family and said several times:

'When you come to Gandumas . . . when you get to know my mother well . . .' The word marriage was never mentioned.

He left for Gandumas the next morning, where he remained a fortnight, and wrote to me frequently. Before returning Philippe sent me the long story of his life with Odile, which I have already spoken about. It interested and surprised me and I discovered in it an anxious and jealous Philippe whom I had never imagined, and also a cynical one at certain crises. I realised that he wanted to give me a true picture of himself in order to avoid any painful surprises. But his self-portrait did not frighten me. What would it matter to me if he were jealous? I should never wish to be unfaithful to him and should not mind his making friends with other women, in fact I would accept anything. His whole behaviour and conversation led me to think that he wanted to marry me. I was very happy and yet a slight anxiety spoilt my pleasure; a shade of annoyance sometimes passed over his face while I was talking or when he watched my movements. This had become more marked and appeared oftener recently. Several times in the course of an evening that began in perfect harmony, I had the impression that he suddenly withdrew into himself at some words of mine and was sad and thoughtful. I tried to reconstruct what I had said. All my remarks seemed to have been harmless. I longed to understand what had shocked him, but could think of nothing. Philippe's reactions seemed to me mysterious and unpredictable.

'Do you know what you ought to do Philippe? Tell me everything that you don't like about me. I know there are things . . . Am I wrong?'

'No – but they are very small things.'

'I should so much like to know what they are and try to correct them.'

'Very well – the next time I go away I will tell you in a letter.'

At the end of the month when he was at Gandumas for two days I received the following:

What I like about you:	*What I don't like:*
You.	Nothing.

What I have just written is true in a sense, but not altogether. Perhaps it would be more accurate to put the same traits in both columns, because there are details that I like as fragments of you but I should not care for them in anyone else. Let's try again:

What I like about you:	*What I don't like:*
Your black eyes, your long eyelashes, the line of your neck and shoulders, your figure.	The rather clumsy stiffness of your gestures, your air of a little girl found guilty.
Above all – a mixture of courage and weakness, boldness and timidity, modesty and ardour. There is something heroic in you; it is very well hidden beneath a lack of will-power in small things, but it is there.	Above all – a refusal to see and accept life as it is; an idealism taken from Anglo-Saxon magazines; an irritating sentimentality. Your severity towards other people's weaknesses.
The young girl side of you.	The old lady side of you.
Your sports clothes.	Your dress with the yellow tunic; the ornaments on your hats (a blue feather), your ochre lace dress; everything superfluous, everything that spoils the line.

What I like about you:	*What I don't like:*
Your conscientious little soul, your simplicity, your tidiness, your well kept books and note-books.	Your economy; your thrifty and sentimental prudence.
Your good-sense.	Your lack of recklessness.
Your modesty.	Your lack of pride.

I could continue for a long time in the left-hand column. All that I put in the right-hand column is not quite accurate. At least I should add:
What I like in you:
What I don't like in you.

Because it is all part of you and I don't wish to transform you, except in quite small things which form a veneer laid over your real self. For instance . . . but I must work a little. Hachette's have asked me to make a special paper for a new publication and a foreman has just come in to submit a sample. How hard it is to tear myself away from a letter to you! One more sentence on the blackboard:
What I like about you:

The long and voluptuous dream I fall into when I begin to think about you

Chamfort relates the following: 'A lady said to the Chevalier de B. "What I like about you . . ." "Oh, Madam!" he interrupted, "if you know what it is, I am lost . . ."'

What I like in you, Isabelle . . .

PHILIPPE

This letter made me feel rather doubtful. I recalled Philippe's critical way of looking at me occasionally. I had noticed for a long time that he attached a curious importance not only to the least of my remarks, but also to my dresses, hats and all the details of my appearance; this saddened, almost humiliated me. I now recognised in myself, to my surprise, certain of my mother's ways of thinking and her instinctive contempt for luxury. Although I understood that Philippe, my hero, was different from me I thought it unworthy of him to care so much about such trivial matters. However, I wanted to please him, and made every effort to become what he seemed to wish me to be. I did not entirely succeed and what worried me most was that I could not see clearly what he wanted. My economy? My lack of recklessness? Yes – it was true. I knew that I was very guarded and cautious. 'How strange it is,' I thought, 'all through my childhood I was romantic, and reacted against the austere matter of fact atmosphere I was brought up in and now Philippe seeing me from the outside, appears to discern in me hereditary features that I thought I was free from.' Reading over again and again what he said, I could not help trying to defend myself; 'Your air of a little girl found guilty . . .' but how could I help it, Philippe? I was treated with a severity that you would find hard to imagine. I could not go out of the house without being accompanied by Mlle Chauvière or my mother . . . Your Odile, Philippe, spent her childhood with indifferent parents who left her free and you suffered greatly in consequence.

'My irritating sentimentality?' . . . it is because I was surrounded by people who had so little feeling that I ask from love a kind caressing atmosphere, which my family had deprived me of . . . 'My modesty? my lack of pride?' . . . How could I be sure of myself when during all my youth I was told of my imperfections and mediocrity? . . .

When Philippe returned I tried to repeat this impassioned defence, but he laughed and was so affectionate that I at once forgot his letter. The date of our marriage was fixed and I was perfectly happy.

My parents came home for the ceremony. They did not dislike Philippe and he liked my father's aloof irony and said that my mother's severe austerity had a poetic 'Marcenat' quality. My family was astonished that we did not have a honeymoon. To see Italy or Greece with Philippe would have been a great joy, but I knew that he did not wish it. I understood what he felt, but my parents attached importance to the conventional demonstrations of happiness and on the day of the wedding my mother predicted a bad future for my marriage.

'Don't give your husband the impression that you love him too much,' she said, 'or you are lost.'

I had now acquired some independence and answered her rather sharply: 'I will look after my happiness myself.'

VI

My happiness during the first three months of our married life is unforgettable. The gradual discovery of love and mutual sympathy! Your delicate kindness and forethought. How harmonious and easy life seemed with you! I wished I could efface all sad and painful thoughts from your mind, give you every possible joy, and sit at your feet. I felt so young and had forgotten my repressed childhood, my hard war work and the perplexity of a woman living alone.

We spent those months at Gandumas, which I liked immensely. I had wanted to know the house and park in which Philippe had grown up. I thought of him as a child and as a little boy, with maternal tenderness. My mother-in-law showed me photographs, schoolboy's exercise books and his curls she had kept. I found her sensible and intelligent. We had many tastes in common, similar fears and tender anxiety for a Philippe who was no longer quite the same as the one she had brought up. She said that Odile's influence had been strong and not good.

'Before his marriage you would never have seen Philippe uneasy or nervous. He had a firm and balanced mind; was greatly interested in his reading and work and resembled his father who was, above all, a slave to duty. Under Odile's influence Philippe became much more . . . difficult. Of course this was only on the surface, his nature was unchanged, but I should not be surprised if you have some trouble at first.'

I made her talk of Odile, whom she had not forgiven for making Philippe unhappy.

'But, Mother,' I said, 'he adored her; he still does; surely that means that she brought him something, in spite of what happened afterwards . . .'

'I think he will be much happier with you and I am grateful, my dear Isabelle.'

We had several conversations that would have seemed strange to a listener overhearing them, because it was I who defended the mythical Odile created and transmitted to me by Philippe.

'You astonish me,' said my mother-in-law. 'You want to make out that you knew Odile better than I did, and yet you had never seen her. I assure you I have nothing but pity for the poor girl, but after all I must tell the truth and describe her to you as I saw her.'

Time passed with alarming speed as though touched by magic. Life seemed to have begun on the day of my marriage.

Before going to the factory in the morning Philippe chose books for me. Some of them, specially those on philosophy, were rather over my head, but if they were about love I read them with pleasure. I copied into a little notebook passages that Philippe had marked in the margins. I liked going with my mother-in-law to the garden-city she had built in memory of her husband on the slopes overlooking the Loue valley. It consisted of a row of clean, hygienic houses that Philippe thought ugly but which were comfortable and convenient. Mme Marcenat had planned in the centre of the village a group of collective institutions that interested me very much. She showed me the domestic school, the hospital and crèche. Owing to my war experience I was able to make suggestions. I had always a liking for organization and order.

I also enjoyed going to the factory with Philippe. In a few days I learnt all about his work which interested me; I liked sitting opposite him in his office piled high with papers of every colour, reading letters from directors of newspapers and publishers or listening to workmen's reports. Sometimes, when all the staff had gone out, I sat on Philippe's knees and he kissed me while looking anxiously towards the door. I noticed with joy that he had an almost constant need of me; as soon as I came near him he took me by the shoulders or round the waist; I discovered that the most completely real person in him was the lover and I found a response in myself I had never suspected before and which now coloured my whole life.

I loved being in that rather wild Limousin country that was impregnated with Philippe. The only place I avoided was the observatory in the park where I knew he had gone with Denise Aubry and later with Odile. I began to feel a strange and retrospective jealousy. Sometimes I wanted to know more. I questioned Philippe about Odile with an almost cruel sharpness. But these moods were fleeting. My only anxiety was my fear of discovering that Philippe was not happy in the same way as I was. That he loved me I could not doubt, but he had not like me a feeling of wonderment and gratitude for this new life.

'Philippe,' I said to him sometimes, 'I want to shout for joy.'

'My God!' he replied, 'how young you are!'

VII

At the beginning of November we returned to Paris. I told Philippe I should like to keep the flat I had occupied in my parents' house.

'There are so many advantages. I pay no rent, the flat is furnished, it is large enough for us both and my parents won't bother us because they only come to Paris for a few weeks in the year. If later they return to France and settle in the rue Ampère there will be time enough to look for something else.'

Philippe refused.

'You are sometimes peculiar, Isabelle. I could not live in that house; it is ugly and in bad taste. The walls and ceilings are plastered all over with unbelievable stuccoes. Your parents would never allow you to make any alterations. No, I assure you, it would be a great mistake . . . I should very much dislike our home . . .'

'Even with me, Philippe? . . . Don't you think people are more important in life than decorations?'

'Of course one can always say that sort of thing and it may sound all right and true . . . But we are lost if you continue in that vein of superficial sentimentality . . . If you say "even with me", I am supposed to answer: "Of course not, my darling," only it would not be true. I know quite well that I should be dissatisfied in that house.'

I gave in, but wanted to take the furniture my parents had given me to Philippe's new flat.

'My poor Isabelle,' he said, 'what is there worth preserving? . . . Perhaps a few bathroom chairs and a kitchen table if you like, and some linen cupboards. All the rest is horrible.'

I was distressed. I knew that none of this furniture was beautiful, but it made me feel at home, and above all it seemed mad to buy new things. I was sure that my mother when she returned would blame me severely, and at heart I should feel she was right.

'But what are we to do with it all then?'

'Why, you must sell it, darling.'

'You know we shall not get a good price; whenever one wants to sell anything, everyone says it is worth nothing.'

'Of course. But it is of no value. For instance that sham Henry II dining-room suite . . . I am astonished, Isabelle, that you should cling to those horrors which you did not even choose yourself.'

'Yes, perhaps I am wrong, Philippe; do as you think best.'

This little scene was re-enacted so often about the most insignificant objects that I ended by laughing about it myself, but in Philippe's red notebook I find the following:

Good Heavens, I know all that is of no importance. Isabelle is so perfect in other ways, and so unselfish. She wants to make everyone round her happy. She has transformed my mother's life at Gandumas . . . Perhaps it is just because she has no marked tastes of her own that she is always trying to guess mine and gratify them. I cannot express a wish in her presence without her coming home in the evening with a parcel containing what I wanted. She spoils me as one spoils a child, as I spoilt Odile. But I feel with sadness and terror that so much amiability only removes her further from me. I reproach myself and fight against it – and can do nothing. I need . . .

what *do* I need? What has happened? I'm afraid what always happens to me: I wanted to embody in Isabelle my Amazon, my Queen, and also in a certain sense Odile, who is now confused in my memory with the Amazon. But Isabelle is not that type of woman. I have cast her for a role she cannot play. What is painful is that I know it and yet try to love her as she is and as she is worthy to be loved, and I suffer. But why, good God, why? I possess that rare blessing, a woman who gives me a great love. I have spent my life in wishing for a romantic love, a successful romance. I have got it and don't want it. I love Isabelle and when I am with her I feel a tender but invincible boredom. Now I understand how I must have bored Odile in the past. This boredom is no reflection on Isabelle and does not prove her to be mediocre and the same could be said of me in relation to Odile. It simply means that the one who is in love is perfectly satisfied to be in the presence of the beloved and therefore has no need or reason to try to fill or enrich the life of either. Yesterday Isabelle and I spent the whole evening in the library. I did not want to read. I should have liked to go out, to see new people, do something. Isabelle, quite happy, raised her eyes from her book every now and again and smiled at me.

Oh, Philippe, dear silent Philippe, why didn't you speak? I already knew so well what you were secretly thinking. No, you would not have hurt my feelings by telling me these things; in fact you might have cured me. Perhaps if we had told each other everything we might have been able to come together again. I knew I was being unwise when I said to you: 'How precious every moment is . . . To go in a car with you, to catch your eye at table, to hear your door bang . . .' It is true my one idea was to be alone with you. To watch and listen to you was enough for me. I had no wish whatever to see new people; I feared them, but if I had known that you had such an intense need of them, perhaps I should have been different.

VIII

Philippe wanted me to meet his friends. I was surprised to find how numerous they were. I don't know why I had imagined and hoped for a more private, more exceptional life. Every Saturday Philippe spent the latter part of the afternoon at Mme de Thianges' house. She seemed to be his most confidential friend and he also liked her sister, Mme Antoine Quesnay very much. This salon was pleasant but rather frightened me. I could not help keeping near Philippe, though I saw that he was rather irritated to find me always in the same group.

All these women received me charmingly, but I did not want to be drawn into their circle. Their ease and self-confidence astonished and embarrassed me; above all I was surprised to find them so intimate with Philippe. There was a comradeship between them that I had never seen anything like in my family. Philippe went out with Françoise Quesnay when she was alone in Paris, or with Yvonne Prévost, the wife of a naval officer, or with a young woman called Thérèse de Saint-Cast who wrote verses and to whom I took a dislike. These outings were apparently quite innocent. Philippe and his friends went to picture exhibitions, in the evenings to films and on Sunday afternoons to concerts. At first he always invited me to join them and sometimes I went, but I did not enjoy myself. On these occasions Philippe was lively and gay as he had formerly been with me. I was hurt at the sight of his pleasure and suffered from his taking an interest in so many different women. A single irresistible passion might have been easier to bear though perhaps more dangerous for my marriage, but at least the misfortune would have been nearer the level of my love. It was painful to see my hero attach so much importance to people who were perhaps agreeable, but whom I thought mediocre. One day I dared to say so:

'Philippe, I should like to understand you. What pleasure do you find in seeing that little Yvonne Prévost? She is not your mistress, you have told me so, and I believe you, but what then does she mean to you? Do you think her intelligent? Personally I find her more boring than anyone.'

'Yvonne? Oh no, she's not boring. You should hear her talk about things she knows. She is the daughter and wife of a sailor; she is familiar with boats and the sea. Last spring I spent a few days with her and her husband on the riviera. We swam and went sailing; it was great fun . . . and she is gay, has a good figure and is pleasant to look at; what more do you want?'

'For you? Much more. I think you are worthy of remarkable women and I see you going about with those who are pretty but insignificant.'

'How unfair and censorious you are! Hélène and Françoise for instance, are both remarkable women and we are very old friends. Before the war, when I was so ill, Hélène was marvellous. She came to look after me, she may even have saved my life . . . You are strange, Isabelle! What is it you want? That I should quarrel with the whole world in order to be alone with you? But I should be sick of it at the end of two days . . . and so would you.'

'Oh no! not I. I am ready to shut myself up with you in a prison for the rest of my days. Only you could not stand it.'

'But nor could you, my poor Isabelle; you wish for an isolated life because you have never tried it – but in reality you would hate it.'

'Just try, darling, and you will see. Listen, Christmas is coming; let us go away alone together. I should enjoy it so much. You know I had no honeymoon.'

'By all means. Where would you like to go?'

'Oh, I don't mind, it doesn't matter so long as I am with you.'

It was agreed that we should spend a few days in the mountains and I at once wrote to St. Moritz to engage rooms.

The idea of this trip made me perfectly happy. But Philippe remained gloomy. He wrote in his notebook:

There is an ironical sadness when one realises how few situations there are in relation to two human beings in this comedy of love. We play in turn the role of the most loved or the least loved. All the answers are the same, though the people who utter them have exchanged their parts. It is now I who see myself at the end of a long day spent away from home, obliged to explain in detail what I have done hour by hour. Isabelle makes an effort to control her jealousy but I am too familiar with the disease to hesitate over the diagnosis. Poor Isabelle! I pity her and cannot cure her. Reflecting on my actual innocence, on the laborious emptiness of the minutes which seem to her so mysterious, I can't help thinking of Odile. What would I not have given in the past if Odile had put so great a value on my actions! But alas! it was just because I cared so much that she attached no importance to what I did.

The longer Isabelle and I live together the more I discover the difference in our tastes. Sometimes in the evening I suggest trying a new restaurant, or going to a cinema or a music-hall. She agrees so mournfully that my evening is spoilt in advance. 'As you don't want to, we won't go. Let's stay here.' 'If it's all the same to you,' she says with relief, 'yes, I should prefer to stay here.'

When we go out with friends my wife's lack of animation chills me; I feel responsible. 'It is curious,' I say to her, 'you are incapable of taking part in an hour's amusement.' 'I find it all so futile,' she says, 'when there are good books on my table or I am behind-hand with work in the house, I feel so strongly that I am wasting my time. But if it amuses you I am quite ready to go out.' 'No,' I reply, rather crossly, 'it no longer amuses me.'

And a few months later I find this:

A summer evening I managed, goodness knows how, to drag Isabelle to the Fair at Neuilly. The merry-go-round organs are playing negro tunes, one hears shots from the rifle-ranges, the clicking of lottery wheels; a hot smell of waffles floats on the air. A packed and slowly moving crowd carries us along. I don't know why, but I am happy; I like this noise and madness; I seem to find here an atmosphere of obscure but true poetry. 'These men and women are being drawn rapidly towards death yet they spend their brief moments throwing a ring over a bottle-neck or making a nigger spring up by a blow from a hammer. And no doubt they are right; in the light of the oblivion that awaits us, I think Napoleon and Richelieu did not use their lives any better than that little woman and her soldier are doing.' I had forgotten Isabelle who was holding my arm. Suddenly she said: 'Let's go home, darling, this tires me horribly.' I called a taxi and as we slowly forced our way through a hostile crowd I thought: 'How charming and gay such an evening would have been with Odile! She would have looked radiant as she did in her happiest moods, would have gambled on all the lotteries and been pleased to win a little glass boat. Poor Odile, who so loved life had such a short one, while creatures made for death, like Isabelle and me, continue our monotonous existence without even wanting it.' Isabelle seemed to guess my thoughts and took my hand. 'Do you feel ill?' I said. 'Oh no – but a Fair bores me so much that it tires me more than anything else.' 'So it bores you, Isabelle? What a pity, when I enjoy it so much.' Then abruptly, and perhaps because at that moment the merry-go-round organ near us was playing a pre-war tune, words Odile had said to me long ago while strolling through this same Fair, came back to me. At that time it was she who reproached me for being bored. Had I then so greatly changed? Just as a house, abandoned by those who built and lived in it, occupied by new masters retains the perfume and even the spirit of the previous owners, I impregnated by Odile, now possessed a soul that was not originally mine. My true preferences, my anxious Marcenat mind had been far nearer to Isabelle's and yet I condemned in her that evening the same severity and distaste for pleasure which were formerly in my own nature and had been effaced from it by another.

IX

The week before we left for the mountains Philippe met at Hélène de Thianges' house the Villiers, a couple he had known in Morocco. It is difficult to find words to describe Mme Villier. She looked proud, even triumphant – She had a clear-cut regular profile, a mass of fair hair, and reminded one of a handsome well-bred animal. As soon as we entered the drawing-room she came towards us:

'M Marcenat and I,' she said, 'went for a wonderful excursion in the Atlas mountains . . . You remember Saïd, Marcenat? . . . Saïd,' she added for my benefit, 'was our guide, a little Arab with sparkling eyes.'

'He was a poet,' said Philippe, 'when we took him with us in the car he sang of the speed of the Roumis and of the beauty of Mme Villier.'

'Won't you take your wife to Morocco this year?' she asked.

'No, we are only going a very short distance – to the mountains. Doesn't that tempt you?'

'Do you mean it? Because, actually, my husband and I wanted to spend Christmas and the New Year in the snow. Whereabouts are you going?'

'To St. Moritz.'

I was furious and made signs to him that he did not see. I ended by getting up and saying:

'We must be going, Philippe.'

'We? Why must we?'

'I've made an appointment at home with the manager.'

'On a Saturday?'

'Yes – I thought it would be more convenient for you.'

He looked at me with surprise but said nothing and got up.

'If you like the idea of this trip,' he said to Mme Villier, 'ring up and we will make arrangements. It would be very amusing for the four of us to go together.'

As we came away he said rather sharply:

'Why the devil did you make an appointment for six o'clock on a Saturday? What a strange idea! You know quite well it is Hélène's day and I like staying there late.'

'I didn't make any appointment Philippe, I just wanted to leave.'

'What an extraordinary thing to do,' he said, bewildered, 'are you ill?'

'No; but I don't want those Villiers to come with us on our holiday. I can't understand your behaviour Philippe. You know quite well that the whole point of this trip for me was our being alone, and then you invite people to join us, almost strangers, whom you have only met once.'

'What passion! What is the matter with you, Isabelle? I have never seen you like this before. You are wrong, I know the Villiers quite well. I stayed a fortnight with them and passed delightful evenings in their garden at Marrakesh. You can't imagine how perfect that house is; the pools and fountains, the four cypresses, the scent of flowers. Solange Villier has exquisite taste. She had arranged it all so well; nothing but Moroccan divans and thick, heavy carpets. Really I was more intimate with the Villiers than with friends in Paris whom one sees three times every winter at dinner parties.'

'Well, perhaps, Philippe, maybe I am quite wrong, but leave me my trip; you promised and you owe it to me.'

Philippe put his hand on mine and laughed:

'Very well, Madam, you shall have your trip.'

The next day, as we drank our coffee together after lunch, Mme Villier rang up Philippe. From his replies, I understood that she had spoken to her husband, he approved of the plan and they would come to Switzerland with us. I gathered that Philippe was not insistent, and he even discouraged them. But his last words were: 'All right, then we shall be delighted to meet you there.'

He replaced the receiver and looked at me with some embarrassment.

'You are a witness,' he said, 'that I did my best.'

'Yes. But still; they are coming? Oh Philippe, it is too bad!'

'But what could I do, darling? I really cannot be insulting.'

'No, but you could have made an excuse; you could have said we were going somewhere else.'

'They would have come there. Anyway, don't make a tragedy about it. They are very nice, you will see, and you will be pleased to have their company.'

'Then listen, Philippe. Just do this: go alone with them. I should not care about coming now.'

'You're crazy! They would not know what to make of it. I think you are most unfair. It was not I who wanted to leave Paris; it was you who asked me to go; I agreed to please you and now you want to make me go alone!'

'Not alone . . . With your dearest friends.'

'Isabelle, I'm sick of this ridiculous scene,' said Philippe angrily. I had never seen him so violent before . . . 'It is not my fault that the Villiers are coming. They invited themselves. In any case they mean nothing to me. I have never made love to Solange . . . I've had enough,' he continued, emphasising each word and striding about the dining-room, 'you are so jealous, so suspicious, that I no longer dare make a movement, say a word . . . Nothing spoils the pleasure of life so much, I assure you . . .'

'What spoils the pleasure of life,' I said, 'is to share it with everyone.'

I listened to myself in astonishment. I knew I was being sarcastic and hostile. I was exasperating the only person in the world I cared for and could not stop myself.

'Poor Isabelle!' he said.

And I, knowing his past life so well and living in his memories perhaps even more than he did himself, knew that he must be thinking:

'Poor Isabelle! Now it is your turn . . .'

I slept very badly that night and kept on reproaching myself. It was certain there was no intimacy between Philippe and Solange Villier as they had not met for a long time. I had no actual grievance nor legitimate cause for jealousy.

Perhaps, even, this meeting was fortunate. Would Philippe have enjoyed himself alone with me at St. Moritz? He might have returned to Paris discontented and under the impression that I had forced him to spend a useless and dull holiday. With the Villiers he would be in good spirits and some of his pleasure would react favourably on me. But I was sad.

X

We were to leave the day before the Villiers but owing to our being delayed we all four went by the same train.

Philippe got up early and when I came out of our compartment I found him standing in the corridor having an animated conversation with Solange. I watched for a moment before approaching them and it struck me how happy they looked.

'Good morning, Mme Villier!' Solange turned round and I could not help wondering if she was like Odile. No, she did not resemble her; she was much more vigorous and her features were less childish and less angelic. Solange looked like a woman who had taken the measure of life and had stood up to it. When she smiled at me I was won over for a moment. Then her husband came to join us.

The train was running between two high mountains and a torrent flowed beside the track. This scenery appeared to me unreal and sad. Jacques Villier talked of boring subjects; I knew he was intelligent because everyone said so. He was not only very successful in Morocco but was also an important business man. 'He is connected with everything,' Philippe told me, 'phosphates, shipping and mines.' I tried to listen to the conversation between Philippe and Solange but the noisy rhythm of the train robbed me of half of it. I heard (Solange's voice): 'Then, what is charm, according to you?' (Philippe's voice): '. . . very complex . . . The face plays a part, and the body . . . but above all naturalness . . .' (a word escaped me, then Solange's voice): 'And also taste, imagination, a spirit of adventure . . . Don't you think so?'

'That's it,' said Philippe, 'a mixture. A woman must be capable of seriousness and childishness . . . What is unbearable . . .'

Once again the noise of the train stole the rest of the sentence. The mountains were rising in front of us. Sawn wood, glistening with resin, was piled up near a châlet with a large sloping roof. Was I going to suffer like this for a whole week?

Jacques Villier ended a long recital by saying:

'. . . you see that the deal is superb, in every way.'

He laughed; no doubt he had explained some ingenious transaction; I only caught a name: 'The Godet group.'

'Superb,' I replied and saw he thought me stupid. I didn't care. I was beginning to hate him.

The end of this journey seems to me now like the recollection of a nightmare. The small overheated train was climbing into a scene of brilliant whiteness while shrouding itself in clouds of steam that floated for an instant over the snow. It followed wide mysterious curves that made the white pine-crowned summits revolve round us. Then a precipice yawned by the side of the track and at the bottom of it one caught sight of the narrow black lines we had just left. Solange watched this sight with childish pleasure and constantly drew Philippe's attention to details of the scenery.

'Look, Marcenat, how beautiful that layer of branches is, holding the snow . . . How one feels the strength of the wood, supporting all that weight without bending . . . And that . . . Oh! . . . look at the hotel shining up there on the peak, like a diamond in a white casket . . . And the colours on the snow . . . Do you notice that it is never just white, but bluish-white, or rose-tinted . . . Oh Marcenat, Marcenat! How I love it!'

There was no harm in this and, honestly, on reflection one had to admit there was a certain grace in the way she said it, but she irritated me. I was surprised that Philippe, who professed to like naturalness above everything, could stand this lyrical monologue.

'Perhaps she does love it,' I thought, 'but really at thirty-three (possibly thirty-five, her neck is not perfect) she can't be so childishly pleased. And we can all see that the snow is blue or pink . . . why say it?' It seemed that Jacques Villier thought as I did because, from time to time he punctuated his wife's sentences with a cynical and long-drawn 'Ye-es'. When he did this I liked him for a moment.

I did not understand the Villier's marriage. They were very polite to each other and she treated him with familiar affection, calling him at times Jacquot or Jacquou and even kissing him on the lips for no apparent reason. And yet, after having passed several hours with them, one knew quite well they were not lovers, that Villier was not jealous and accepted his wife's adventures in advance with a lofty resignation. What did he live for? For another woman? For his mines, his boats and his estate in Morocco? I could not guess and anyway was not sufficiently interested to care. I despised him for being so indulgent. 'He doesn't want to be here any more than I do,' I thought, 'and if he had a little more strength of mind neither of us would be.'

Philippe who had bought a Swiss paper tried to work out the Stock Exchange prices in French francs and thinking to please Villier, talked to him of certain securities. Villier calmly passed over these strange names of Mexican or Greek factories, as a famous writer makes a deprecating gesture when a flatterer quotes his works. Turning to me, he asked if I had read *Koenigsmark*. The little train was still winding amongst soft white shapes.

Why does St. Moritz stay in my memory like the scene of

a comedy by Alfred de Musset, gay, unreal and with a suggestion of deep melancholy? I remember so well going from the station into the darkness, the lights on the snow, the sleighs, mules with bells and red, blue or yellow pom-poms on their harnesses, the cruel but healthy cold, then the marvellous comforting warmth of the hotel; Englishmen in dinner-jackets in the hall, the happiness of being alone with Philippe at last, for a few minutes in the mild temperature of our enormous room.

'Philippe, kiss me, we must consecrate this room . . . Oh how I should have liked to dine here alone with you . . . And we shall have to dress, rejoin those people and talk and talk . . .'

'But they are very nice . . .'

'Very nice . . . as long as one doesn't see them.'

'How severe you are! Didn't you think Solange was very pleasant during the journey?'

'Look here, Philippe, you are in love with her.'

'Good heavens no! Why do you think so?'

'Because unless you were in love with her you couldn't stand her for ten minutes . . . After all, what did she say? Can you tell me of a single idea in all her talk since this morning?'

'Why yes . . . She has a great feeling for nature. She spoke very charmingly of the snow and the pine trees . . . Don't you think so?'

'Oh yes, she can put things picturesquely at times; but so can I and all women if we let ourselves go . . . It is our natural way of thinking . . . The great difference between Solange and me is that I think much too highly of you to tell you all that passes through my head.'

'My dear girl,' Philippe said, with affectionate irony, 'I have never doubted your ability to invent pretty phrases nor the modesty that prevents you from uttering them.'

'Don't laugh at me darling . . . I am serious . . . If you were not a little charmed by Solange you would see that she is incoherent and jumps from one subject to another . . . Isn't that true? Be sincere.'

'It is not true at all,' said Philippe.

XI

I look back upon that visit to the mountains as a cruel and bitter experience. I knew already of my natural awkwardness and inefficiency at all kinds of sport but thought Philippe and I would start as beginners and enjoy overcoming the difficulties together. The first morning I discovered that Solange Villier was an expert performer on the ice. Philippe, though less trained, was supple and very much at his ease. They skated happily with crossed hands while I dragged myself painfully along, supported by an instructor.

After dinner Philippe and Solange drew their chairs close to each other and chatted all the evening while I had to listen to the financial views of Jacques Villier. At this time the pound was worth sixty francs and I remember his saying:

'You know, that is far from representing the actual value of the pound; you ought to tell your husband to invest at least part of his capital in foreign securities because, you understand . . .'

Sometimes he talked of his love affairs: 'You have probably heard that Jenny Sorbier, the actress, is my mistress. It is no longer true . . . I loved her very much, but it is over . . . Now I am with Mme Lhauterie . . . Do you know her? She is a pretty woman and very sweet. A man who has to struggle unceasingly as I do with his business life, needs a calm, almost animal-like affection from women . . .'

I was manoeuvring to get near Philippe and to start a general conversation. When I succeeded it was immediately evident that Solange and I held opposite and irreconcilable opinions on every subject. Her principal theme was 'adventure'. She called the search for unexpected and dangerous situations by this name and pretended to have a horror of either moral or physical well-being.

'I am glad to be a woman,' she said one evening, 'because there are far more possibilities for a woman than for a man.'

'But how can that be? A man has his career – he can do things.'

'A man has *one* career – whereas a woman can live in the lives of all the men she loves. An officer teaches her about war, a sailor about the sea, from a diplomat she learns of intrigue, from a writer the pleasures of creation . . . She can feel the emotions of ten existences without the daily tedium of living them.'

'But how dreadful! That implies that she loves ten different men.'

'And that all ten are intelligent, which is very unlikely,' said Villier, strongly emphasising the word *very*.

'One could say the same of men,' said Philippe. 'The successive women they love bring them a variety of lives also.'

'Yes, perhaps,' said Solange, 'but women are so much less individual; they have nothing much to bring.'

One day a remark of hers struck me very much by the tone in which it was uttered. She had spoken of the happiness one feels in escaping from civilisation and I said:

'But why escape, if one is happy in it?'

'Because happiness is never stable; it is the relief from anxiety.'

'Quite true,' said Villier, and this surprised me, coming from him.

Then Philippe, to please Solange, returned to the theme of evasion:

'Oh yes, – to escape . . . that would be delightful.'

'For you?' said Solange. 'You are the last person who would really wish to escape.'

This pained me for his sake. Solange rather liked to sting men's vanity with a crack of the whip, so to speak. Whenever Philippe showed me affection or said a kind word to me, she was sarcastic. But most of the time they behaved like an engaged couple.

Every morning Solange came down in a new brightly coloured jumper and each time Philippe murmured: 'Good heavens, what taste you have!'

Towards the end of our visit he had become very intimate with her. What upset me most was the familiar and affectionate tone in which they spoke to each other and the caressing way he helped her on with her coat. Solange was terribly cat-like, I can find no other word. When she came down in a low-cut evening dress I could almost see electric waves running down her spine. As we returned to our room I could not help saying, without bitterness:

'So you love her Philippe.'

'Who, darling?'

'Solange, of course.'

'O Lord, no!'

'And yet you appear to.'

'Do I,' he said, with ill-concealed pleasure. 'In what way?'

I explained my impressions at length; he listened complacently. He was always interested when I talked about Solange.

'All the same, they are a curious married couple,' I said, shortly before we left. 'Villier has told me that he spends six months of the year in Morocco and his wife joins him there every other year and then only for three months. She stays alone in Paris for whole seasons. If you had to live in Indo-China or Kamchatka I should follow you everywhere, like a little dog . . . I should bore you to death, shouldn't I Philippe? No doubt she is quite right.'

'That is to say she has found the best way to avoid wearying him.'

'A lesson for Isabelle?'

'How touchy you are. No – it's not a lesson for anyone, but a statement of fact. Villier adores his wife . . .'

'That is what *she* tells you, Philippe . . .'

'Anyway he admires her.'

'And doesn't look after her.'

'Why should he?' said Philippe rather irritably. 'I have never heard that she needs looking after.'

'Oh Philippe! I have only known her for three weeks and have already heard the names of at least three of her former lovers mentioned.'

'People say that about all women,' murmured Philippe, shrugging his shoulders.

I felt I was falling into a despicable frame of mind, which was entirely new to me. I took myself in hand and made a great effort to be nice to Solange. Against my will I went for walks with Villier so as to leave her alone on the skating rink with Philippe. How passionately I longed for this holiday to be over but scrupulously avoided saying a word to hasten its end.

XII

When we returned to Paris Philippe found his manager ill, had to work harder than usual and often did not come home for lunch. I wondered if he were seeing Solange Villier but did not dare to ask him. On Saturdays at the Thianges' when Solange was there, Philippe went straight to join her as soon as he arrived and drew her into a corner where they remained together the rest of the evening. That could be a favourable sign. If they had been meeting freely during the week he might have purposely avoided her on Saturdays.

I could not resist talking about her to other women, but never spoke against her. She had the reputation of being 'une grande amoureuse'. One evening I was standing beside Maurice de Thianges, and when Jacques Villier came in, he said in an undertone:

'Hallo! So he hasn't gone away yet? I should have thought his wife would already have sent him back to his Atlas Mountains!'

Whoever mentioned him, usually added: 'Poor fellow!'

Hélène de Thianges was a friend of Solange's and talked at length about her to me. She gave me a picture that was both flattering and disquieting.

'First of all,' she said, 'Solange is a beautiful animal, and with very strong instincts. She was passionately in love with Villier when he was very poor, because he was handsome. This showed courage, as she was the daughter of a Count de Vaulges who belonged to a good Picardy family; she was lovely and could have made a brilliant match. She preferred to go off with Villier to Morocco where at first they lived the hard life of the settler. When Villier was ill, Solange had to keep the books and pay the workmen herself. Remember, she has the proud spirit of the Vaulges and such a life must have been distasteful to her. Yet she played the game. In that respect she really has the merits of a good man. Only she has two great faults, or, if you like, two great weaknesses; she is extremely passionate and she must conquer wherever she goes. For instance she says (not to men but to women) that when she wanted a man she always got him, and it's true, even men of the most varied types.'

'Then has she had many lovers?'

'It is very difficult to be certain of such things. One knows that a man and woman see a lot of each other. Are they lovers? Who can tell? . . . When I say she "got them", I mean that she took possession of their minds, they depended on her and she could do whatever she liked with them.'

'Do you think she is intelligent?'

'Yes, very intelligent for a woman . . . In fact nothing is foreign to her. Naturally she depends for her subjects of interest on the man she loves. At the time when she adored her husband she was brilliant about economic and colonial questions; at the Raymond Berger period she was interested in art. She has very good taste. Her house in Morocco is a marvel and the one at Fontainebleau most original . . . She is more a lover than an intellectual. All the same she has admirable judgement when she keeps her head.'

'How do you explain her charm, Hélène?'

'I think it comes first of all from her being so feminine.'

'What do you mean by feminine?'

'A mixture of qualities and faults; tenderness and a great devotion to the man she loves . . . for a time . . . She is also unscrupulous . . . When Solange wants to make a conquest she is ruthless, cares for no-one, not even her best friend; she is not wicked, but instinctive.'

'I call that wicked. You might as well say that a tiger is not wicked when he eats a man, because it is instinctive.'

'Exactly; a tiger is not wicked, not consciously so . . . What you have just said is very true: Solange is a tigress.'. .

'Yet she looks very sweet.'

'Do you think so? Oh no – there are flashes of hardness; it is one of the elements of her beauty.'

The other women were less indulgent. Old Mme de Thianges, Hélène's mother-in-law, said:

'No, I don't like your little friend Mme Villier . . . She made one of my nephews very unhappy; he was a charming fellow, he really let himself be killed during the war, not for her perhaps, but on account of her . . . He had been seriously wounded and had quite rightly been given a post in Paris . . . She made him love her, drove him mad, then left him for another . . . Poor Armand wanted to go back to the front and was killed, uselessly, in a flying accident . . . Personally I don't want to receive her any more.'

I had no intention of repeating these stories to Philippe and yet I always did. He took them calmly.

'Yes, it is possible she has had lovers,' he said. 'She has the right and it is no concern of ours.'

Then after a few minutes he became nervous:

'In any case I should be very surprised if she were being unfaithful to Villier at present as she leads such an open life. One can telephone to her at almost any hour; she is at home a lot and if one wants to see her she is always free. A woman who had a lover would be much more secretive.'

'But how do you know Philippe? Do you ring her up? Do you go to see her?'

'Yes, sometimes.'

XIII

A little later I was able to prove that though they had long conversations on the telephone together, these conversations were innocent. One morning after Philippe had left, a letter arrived that I could not answer without consulting him, and I rang up his office. The lines were crossed and I recognised the voices of Solange and Philippe. I ought to have replaced the receiver, but could not resist listening. They sounded gay; Philippe seemed amusing and witty as he used to be but never was now. I preferred him serious and melancholy, as Renée described him long ago and as I knew him just after the war. But I also knew the very different Philippe who was at this moment saying pleasant, frivolous things to Solange. All that I heard was reassuring. They were telling each other what they had done and read in the last two days. Philippe described the play we had seen together the night before and Solange asked:

'Did Isabelle like it?'

'Yes – I think so – rather . . . How are you? You didn't look well on Saturday at the Thianges; I don't like to see you so pale.'

So they had not met since the previous Saturday and this was Wednesday. Suddenly I felt ashamed and put down the receiver. How could I have done such a mean thing? It was as bad as opening other peoples' letters.

A quarter of an hour later I rang up Philippe:

'I called you a little while ago,' I said, 'but you were engaged. I recognised Solange's voice and rang off.'

'Yes,' he answered, without embarrassment, 'she telephoned to me.'

This whole episode seemed to me very clear and straightforward, and I felt calmer for a time. Then I again found obvious signs of Solange's influence on Philippe's life. He now went out two or three evenings a week; I did not ask where he went but knew he had been seen with her. She had enemies amongst women who, thinking I would be their natural ally, tried to approach me. Those who were nice (that is to say as nice as women can be to each other) treated me with silent pity and made no allusion to my misfortune except in general terms; those who were spiteful pretended they thought I was aware of facts I knew nothing about. One woman said:

'I quite understand your not wanting to go and see acrobats with your husband; they are such a bore.'

'Did Philippe go to see acrobats?' I asked, curiosity getting the better of my pride.

'Didn't he tell you that he was at the Alhambra last night with Solange Villier? I thought you knew.'

Men pretended to sympathise with me in order to offer consolation.

If we had an invitation for dinner or if I suggested some outing, Philippe often replied:

'Yes, why not? But wait till tomorrow before deciding, I'll let you know then.'

My explanation for this delay was that Philippe wanted to ring up Solange in the morning and find out if she was going to the same dinner or whether she wanted to go out with him that evening.

It seemed to me that Philippe's tastes, even his character, now showed Solange's influence. She liked the country and gardens and knew about plants and animals. She had a bungalow built near Fontainebleau on the edge of the forest and often went there for week-ends. Philippe said several times that he was tired of Paris and would like to have a little place on the outskirts.

'But you have Gandumas, Philippe, and you hardly ever go there.'

'It is not the same thing at all; Gandumas is seven hours from Paris. I should like a house I could run down to for a couple of days – or even for the day. For instance Chantilly, or Compiègne or St. Germain.'

'Or Fontainebleau, Philippe.'

'Or Fontainebleau if you like,' he said, smiling involuntarily.

I almost liked that smile; it seemed to take me into his confidence, as if to say: 'Yes, of course you know and I trust you.'

I felt however that I must not go too far as he would never tell me anything definite; I was sure that Solange was the source of Philippe's sudden love of nature and that his plans depended largely on hers. It was equally remarkable to trace his influence on her tastes. I who was usually so unobservant did not miss the smallest details concerning those two.

On Saturdays at Hélène's I often heard Solange talking about books. Now she read those that Philippe liked and had made me read. Sometimes they were books François had formerly introduced to Odile and she had passed on to Philippe. I was familiar with this bold and cynical 'legacy' from François. It included Cardinal de Retz and Machiavelli. Then there was Philippe's choice: *Lucien Leuwen*, *Smoke* by Turgenev and the first volumes of Proust. The day I heard Solange talking of Machiavelli I knew quite well, being myself a woman, that she was as indifferent to him as she would be to ultra-violet rays or Limoges enamels, though she could show an interest and talk intelligently of either if she thought she could please a man by doing so.

When I first knew Solange I noticed her love for bright colours which suited her well. But recently I saw her nearly always wearing a white dress in the evening. White was one of Philippe's preferences, inherited from Odile. How often he had spoken of her brilliant whiteness! It was strange that poor little Odile continued to live for Philippe in other women. Solange and I (Solange perhaps unconsciously) tried to reproduce a semblance of her vanished grace. What made me suffer most, apart from my acute jealousy, was the thought that Philippe was unfaithful to Odile's memory. When I first met him I regarded this fidelity as one of the finest traits in his character. Later when I read the story of his life with Odile and learned that she had deserted him for another man I admired Philippe still more for his reverence for the memory of the only woman he had loved. I understood it all the better because through his description I had formed a wonderful image of Odile, her fragile beauty and naturalness and her poetic imagination. In spite of my jealousy I loved her. She alone appeared worthy of the Philippe I had conceived. I was willing to be sacrificed to such a noble love and accepted defeat by Odile with perhaps a secret pride in my humility. But this sentiment was not as pure as it seemed for was I not hoping that Philippe's everlasting love for a being, who through death had become almost holy in his eyes, might prevent his being the slave of a Solange Villier who was a creature of flesh and blood like myself, neither divine nor superhuman?

XIV

Philippe said several times: 'Solange has done her best to become more friendly with you, but you always keep her at a distance. She feels that you are hostile and strange . . .'

Mme Villier had often telephoned to me since our trip to Switzerland but I refused to go out with her. I thought it more creditable not to see much of her. All the same to please Philippe and prove my good will, I promised to go and see her once.

She received me in a small boudoir arranged according to Philippe's taste; very empty, almost bare. I was embarrassed. Solange stretching herself with light-hearted ease on a divan, began talking in a confidential tone. She called me Isabelle whilst I wavered between 'Mme Villier' and 'chère amie'.

How curious it is that Philippe who had such a horror of familiarity and of lack of modesty, was so drawn to this woman who had no reserve and said whatever entered her head. Why did he like her? . . . There was a certain tenderness in her eyes . . . she seemed happy . . . Was she really?

The picture of Villier, with his slightly bald head, and the sound of his tired voice, crossed my mind. I asked for news of him. He was absent, as usual.

'I see very little of Jacques you know,' said Solange, 'but he is my best friend. He is so straight, so frank . . . Only after thirteen years of married life, it would be hypocritical to maintain the fiction of a great love . . . which I don't feel.'

'Yet you married for love, didn't you?'

'Yes, I adored Jacques. We had some beautiful moments together. But passion never lasts long . . . And then the war separated us. After four years we got so accustomed to living apart . . .'

'How sad! And you have not tried to rebuild your happiness?'

'Well, you know, when people don't love each other any more . . . or more precisely, when there is no longer any physical attraction (because I am still very fond of Jacques), it is difficult to remain outwardly a united couple . . . I know Jacques has a mistress and I approve . . . You can't understand that yet, but the moment comes when one needs independence . . .'

'Why? To me, marriage and independence are contradictory terms.'

'One says that at first. But marriage as you conceive it has a disciplinary side. Are you shocked?'

'A little . . . that's to say . . .'

'I am very frank, Isabelle. I hate pretence. In pretending to love Jacques . . . or to hate him, I might gain your sympathy but I would not be myself . . . Do you understand?'

She talked without looking at me while drawing little stars on the cover of a book. When her eyes were lowered her face looked rather hard and as if stamped with obscure suffering.

'She is not really so happy,' I thought.

'No,' I said, 'I don't quite understand . . . A chaotic, desultory life must be so unsatisfying . . . And then you have a son.'

'Yes; but you will see for yourself how it is when you have children. There is no interchange possible between a woman and a schoolboy of twelve. When I go and see him he seems bored.'

'So, according to you maternal love is also unreal?'

'Oh no . . . it all depends on the circumstances . . . You are rather aggressive, Isabelle!'

'What I don't understand about you is that while saying "I am frank, I accept no hypocrisy," you have never dared to go to extreme lengths . . . Your husband has taken back his independence, he gives you complete liberty . . . why don't you get divorced? It would be more straightforward and definite.'

'What a strange idea! I don't want to marry again, neither does Jacques, so why should we have a divorce? Besides, we have interests in common. Our land in Marrakesh was bought with my dowry but it is Jacques who has developed it and increased its value . . . And I am always very glad to see him again . . . All this is more complex than you think, dear Isabelle.'

Then she told me about her Arab horses, her pearls and her hothouses at Fontainebleau. She says she despises luxury, that her real life is on a different level, yet she can't resist talking about her possessions . . . Perhaps it is this childish enjoyment of material things that charms Philippe . . . All the same it is amusing to notice the difference of tone between her lyrical monologues when a man is present and the inventory of her goods, with which she hopes to impress a woman.

When I left she said, laughing:

'No doubt I have shocked you, because you have been married such a short time and are in love . . . All that is charming. But don't dramatise things . . . Philippe loves you and speaks very affectionately of you.'

To be reassured by Solange with regard to my marriage and Philippe's feelings towards me was intolerable. She added:

'Goodbye for the present: come and see me again.'

I never returned.

XV

A few weeks after this visit I felt ill, had a cough and was shivering. Philippe spent the evening at my bedside. The half-light and perhaps the fever gave me courage to speak of the change I had noticed in his behaviour.

'You can't see yourself, Philippe, but to me it is almost incredible . . . Even the things you say . . . The other evening when you were arguing with Maurice de Thianges it struck me you were so hard in your judgements.'

'Good Heavens! How attentive you are to everything I say, my poor Isabelle; far more than I am, myself, I assure you. What did I say that was so terrible?'

'I have always admired your ideas about loyalty, keeping promises, and respect for undertakings, but this time you may remember it was Maurice who upheld these views and you said life is short, men are unfortunate creatures who have few opportunities for happiness and should seize those that are offered; and then Philippe . . .' (I looked away from him to say this). 'It seemed to me that you were talking for the benefit of Solange, who was listening.'

Philippe laughed and took my hand.

'How feverish you are and what an imagination you have! No, of course I was not talking for Solange. What I said was true. We tie ourselves up, nearly always without knowing what we are doing. Then we want to be honest; we don't want to hurt those we love and for confused reasons we deny ourselves definite pleasures, and regret it afterwards. I said that there is a cowardly kindness in this and as we are usually resentful towards those for whom we have renounced pleasures, it is better for them and for us that we should follow our impulses and face the consequences.'

'But is there something you regret at this moment, Philippe?'

'You always apply general questions to ourselves. No I regret nothing; I love you very much and am perfectly happy with you, but I should be even happier if you were not jealous.'

'I will try not to be.'

The next day the doctor came and found I had a bad attack of tonsilitis. Philippe stayed with me constantly and watched over my treatment with great devotion. Solange sent me flowers and books and came to see me as soon as I was allowed visitors. I felt I had been unjust and horrid, but when I was well and began to lead a normal life again I was struck even more by the intimacy between Philippe and Solange and my suffering returned. Nor was I the only one to be concerned. M Schreiber, the manager of the paper-works often came to lunch with us and inspired me with great confidence. One day when I had gone to see Philippe at his office and found that he was not there, M Schreiber drew me aside and said:

'Please forgive me for asking you a question, but do you know what is the matter with M Philippe? He is no longer the same man.'

'In what way?'

'He is indifferent to everything; seldom returns to the office in the afternoons, and misses appointments with his best clients; it is three months since he went to Gandumas . . . I do my best, but I am not the chief . . . I cannot take his place.'

So when Philippe told me he was occupied with his business he was sometimes lying; he, who had always been so loyal and so scrupulous. But was he not lying to reassure me? And did I make sincerity easy for him? Sometimes, wanting him to be happy, I vowed not to disturb his peace, but more often I plagued him with questions and reproaches. I was bitter, persistent and hateful. He answered with great patience. It occurred to me that he had been kinder to Odile in similar circumstances than I was to him; but I excused myself because I considered that the situation was much more terrible for me than it had been for him.

A man does not stake his whole life on love; he has his work, his friends and his ideas. A woman of my kind lives only for the man she loves. What could replace him? I detested women and was indifferent to men. After waiting so long I thought I had at last achieved the only aim I ever had in life, to give and receive complete devotion. I had failed. There was no remedy or consolation for such a cruel blow.

Thus the second year of my marriage went by.

XVI

Meanwhile two events occurred that reassured me. For a long time Philippe had intended going to America to study certain processes connected with his factory and the living conditions of American workmen. I was anxious to go with him. From time to time he made plans, sent me to enquire about boat sailings and the price of tickets; then, after prolonged hesitation, he would decide not to go. I ended by thinking we should never take the journey but in any case resigned myself in advance to everything. I now adopted Philippe's ideas about chivalrous love. I loved him and always would, whatever happened, but should never be perfectly happy.

One evening in January 1922 Philippe said:

'This time I have decided; we will go to the United States in the spring.'

'I too, Philippe?'

'Of course. It is largely because I promised to take you that I want to go. We will stay there six weeks. My business will be finished in a week and we can travel about and see the country.'

'How good you are, Philippe! I am delighted.'

I really thought it was good of him; lack of self-confidence brings with it a deep and naïve humility. I sincerely believed that Philippe could not find much pleasure in travelling with me, and felt grateful that he was willing to renounce all possibility of seeing Solange Villier for two months. If he loved her as much as I sometimes feared, he would never have left her for so long. Therefore the affair must be less serious than I had thought. During all that month of January I was gay and light-hearted and did not once bother Philippe with complaints and questions.

In February I realised I was going to have a baby. This made me very happy. I had longed passionately for a child, specially a son; I thought he would be another Philippe but this time would belong to me completely for fifteen years at least. Philippe welcomed the news with joy, which gratified me deeply. But the beginning of my pregnancy was very hard and it was soon evident that I should not be able to stand the sea journey. Philippe offered to give up the trip. I knew he had already written many letters, arranged visits to factories and made appointments so I insisted that he should not alter his plans. There were several reasons for my imposing this painful separation on myself. To begin with I thought I looked ugly at that period; my face was tired and I was afraid of appearing unattractive to Philippe. Also it seemed even more important to keep him and Solange apart, than to have him with me. Finally I had often heard Philippe express the view that a woman's great power lies in her absence; when a man is far away from her he forgets her defects and whims and discovers that she brings a precious, indispensable element into his life, which he had not been aware of before, owing to their lives being so closely intermingled. 'It is like salt,' he said, 'We don't even know we are absorbing it, but remove it altogether from our food and we should die.'

If only Philippe, far away from me, would discover that I was the salt of his life . . .

He left at the beginning of April, and advised me to occupy myself and to see people. After a few days, feeling better, I tried to go out a little. I could not expect a letter from him for a fortnight and felt the need of shaking off the melancholy that was getting a hold on me. I telephoned to several friends and thought it would be correct and tactful to ring up Solange.

I had great difficulty in getting a reply; at last a man-servant told me she had gone away for two months. This gave me a violent shock. I was foolish enough to think she had gone with Philippe, which was most unlikely. I asked for her address and was told she was at her house in Marrakesh. Of course, she was making her usual visit to Morocco. After this I had to lie on my bed, feeling very upset and spent a long time in sad reflections. So that was why Philippe had been so ready to go on this journey . . . I was angry with him for not telling me the truth and allowing me to accept his offer as a generous sacrifice. Today, with the passing of time, I feel more indulgent. Unable to tear himself away from

Solange, yet being fond of me, he had done his best to give me all he could spare from a passion that was becoming only too evident.

The first letters I received from America removed this unpleasant impression. They were affectionate and vivid; he seemed to regret my absence and wished he could share with me the life he was enjoying. He wrote:

This country would suit you, Isabelle, it is a country of comfort and perfection, well organised and everything is well done. New York might be a giant house directed by an efficient and all-powerful Isabelle.

And in another letter:

How I miss you, my darling! How much I should like to find you here in the evening in this hotel bedroom, empty except for a too active telephone. We should have one of our long enjoyable conversations, talk over the people and events of the day and your clear little mind would make valuable suggestions. Then you would say, no doubt with hesitation and assumed indifference: 'Do you really think she is pretty, that Mrs Cooper Lawrence you were talking to all the evening?' And I should kiss you and we should look at each other and laugh. Isn't that true, darling?

In reading his letter I felt truly grateful to him for knowing me so well and accepting me.

XVII

Everything in life is unexpected and perhaps this is so until the end. The separation which I had dreaded proved to be a time of relative happiness. I was rather lonely, but read and worked. In any case I was very tired and slept part of the day. Illness can give us a kind of moral well-being as it imposes definite limits to our desires and cares. Philippe was far away but I knew he was well and in good spirits. He wrote me charming letters and there was no quarrel or shadow between us. Solange was in the remotest part of Morocco separated from my husband by a sea voyage of seven or eight days. The world seemed more beautiful, and life easier and calmer than it had been for a long time. I now understood something Philippe had said which I considered monstrous at the time:

'Love bears absence and death better than doubt or treachery.'

Philippe had made me promise to see our friends. I dined once at the Thianges and two or three times with Aunt Cora, who had aged very much and sometimes fell asleep in her chair. Her collection of admirals, generals and ambassadors had been greatly reduced by death. I always remembered gratefully that she had introduced Philippe to me and I continued to visit her, even lunched alone with her on several occasions. One day I began to confide in her, talked first about my childhood, then of my marriage and of my jealousy of Solange. She smiled as she listened.

'Well, my dear, if you never have worse misfortunes you will be a lucky woman . . . What are you complaining of? Your husband is unfaithful? Husbands are never faithful . . . Do you imagine my poor Adrian was always faithful to me? My dear Isabelle, during twenty years of my life I knew that my best friend was his mistress . . . I won't pretend that this was always pleasant but everything settled down . . . I remember the day of our golden wedding . . . Adrian made a little speech in which, growing rather confused, he spoke of me and of her at the same time . . . people laughed, but it was really very touching; we were old and had spent our lives as well as we could and nothing had been spoilt beyond repair . . .'

'Yes, but it depends on one's nature. For me it is the emotional side of life that matters. I am indifferent to worldly considerations.'

'But who says you should have no emotional life? Naturally I am very fond of my nephew and it would not be correct for me to advise you to take a lover . . . but if you chose to console yourself with someone else . . .'

Aunt Cora and I liked each other very much but there could be no real understanding between us.

I was invited to dinner by the Sommervieus, business acquaintances of Philippe's, and thought it my duty to accept. My hostess introduced me to various people; the women were mostly pretty and covered with beautiful jewels, the men were nearly all of the engineer type, robust and energetic.

I heard the names M and Mme Godet and saw an important looking man with a pretty rather faded blonde. The name seemed familiar. 'Who is M Godet?' I asked my hostess.

'He is the big man in metallurgy, the administrator of Western Steel Works and very powerful in the mining industry.'

He sat next to me at table and I saw him looking at my card with curiosity.

'Are you by any chance Philippe Marcenat's wife?'

'Yes, indeed I am.'

'I knew your husband well. It was with him, or rather with his father that I began my career at Limousin. I had to deal with a paper factory which did not interest me. Your father-in-law was a severe man, difficult to work with . . . I must admit that Gandumas is an unhappy memory for me.'

While he was talking I suddenly understood . . . This was Misa's husband. All Philippe's story came back to me as clearly as if the sentences were before my eyes. So it was that pretty woman at the end of the table, with the soft, plaintive eyes, smiling gaily at her neighbour whom Philippe had embraced one evening as they sat together on cushions before a dying fire. I could hardly believe it. I had imagined Misa a cruel, voluptuous woman with the appearance and air of a Lucrezia Borgia or a Hermione. Why had Philippe given me such a bad description of her? But now I had to talk to her husband.

'Yes, I have often heard about you from Philippe.' Then I added a little nervously:

'I believe Mme Godet was a great friend of my husband's first wife?'

He stopped looking at me and seemed rather confused. I wondered how much he knew.

'Yes, they were friends from childhood. Then there were difficulties. Odile did not behave very well to Misa . . .'

Seeing that he was embarrassed I changed the subject and he talked of his industrial and political interests.

After dinner I managed to be alone with his wife. I knew Philippe would not have approved of this but a passionate curiosity impelled me to approach her. She seemed surprised. I said:

'Your husband reminded me at dinner that you once knew mine very well.'

'Yes,' she said coldly, 'Julien and I lived at Gandumas for some months.'

She looked at me in a peculiar way, both questioning and sad, as if she were wondering whether I knew the truth and if my apparent amiability was assumed. Strangely enough I did not dislike her, in fact I found her sympathetic. Her grace and her serious melancholy expression touched me. She appeared to have suffered deeply. Perhaps she had really loved Philippe and, desiring his happiness, warned him against a woman who could only bring him sorrow. Was that such a crime?

I sat down beside Misa and tried to draw her out. After an hour she began to talk about Odile. She could not do so without a certain embarrassment, which showed how acute the feelings revived by this conversation had been and still were.

'It is very difficult for me to speak of Odile,' she said. 'I greatly loved and admired her. Later she treated me badly and then she died. I don't want to sully her name, especially to you.'

She looked at me again in that strange questioning way.

'Don't imagine I am hostile to her memory,' I said. 'I have heard Odile talked about so much that I almost consider her as part of myself. She must have been so beautiful.'

'Yes,' she said sadly, 'she was wonderfully beautiful. Yet there was something about her eyes I did not like. Something false . . . no – that would be too much . . . it was, I don't know how to put it . . . a kind of triumphant cunning. She wanted to impose *her* will, *her* truth on others. Her beauty gave her self-confidence and she believed, almost in good faith, that if she stated something it would become true. With your husband, who adored her, it succeeded, but not with me, and she resented this.'

I felt distressed; I was re-discovering the Odile of Renée and my mother-in-law almost the Solange of Hélène de Thianges, and no longer Philippe's Odile, who was the one I loved.

'But how extraordinary,' I said, 'you are describing someone strong and wilful. When Philippe talks about her I have the impression of a fragile, delicate woman, always lying down, rather childish, but at heart very good.'

'Yes – that was true in a way – but the real Odile had the audacity of . . . I don't really know how to tell you . . . the audacity of a soldier or a partisan. For instance, when she wanted to hide . . . but no, I don't want to speak about that.'

'What you call audacity Philippe calls courage; he said it was one of her finest qualities.'

'Yes – maybe, but she had not the courage to set limits to her actions. She had the courage to carry out her own wishes; that also is fine, but less difficult.'

'Have you any children,' I asked.

'Yes,' she said, looking down, 'two boys and a girl.'

We talked all the evening and when we said goodbye the beginning of a friendship had been sketched. For the first time I was in complete disagreement with Philippe's judgement. No, this woman was not malicious; she had been in love and jealous. What right had I to blame her? At the last moment I had an impulse which I regretted later. I said:

'Perhaps we could go out together sometime? I have enjoyed talking to you and I am alone at present.'

As soon as I left the room I knew I had been wrong and that when Philippe heard I had made friends with Misa he would be very angry and no doubt quite rightly.

She also must have found a certain pleasure in our conversation, or perhaps she was curious about me and my marriage, for she rang me up two days later and we arranged to go for a walk in the Bois. What I wanted was to make her talk of Odile, to learn about her tastes, habits and ways and thus perhaps become more pleasing to Philippe myself. I never dared question him about the past. I asked Misa many things:

'How did Odile dress? Where did she get her hats? I have been told she arranged flowers so well . . . how can the arrangement of flowers be so personal? Explain to me . . . How strange it is, you and everyone tell me she had such charm, yet certain details you mention reveal her as hard, almost unpleasant. What then did her charm consist of?'

But as to this Misa was incapable of giving me the least idea and I saw that she herself had often been puzzled by this question and had never discovered the answer. She could only tell me about Odile's feeling for nature, which Solange also had, and her spontaneous vivacity, which I lacked. I am too methodical and mistrust my own bursts of enthusiasm. I decided it must have been the childish side of Odile, and her gaiety that charmed Philippe more than her moral qualities.

Then we started talking more intimately about Philippe. I told Misa how much I loved him.

'Yes,' she said, 'but are you happy with him?'

'Very happy. Why do you ask?'

'For no reason – I just wondered. And I quite understand how fond you are of him; he is so lovable. But at the same time he has such a weakness for women of the Odile type that he must be a difficult husband.'

'Why do you say women? Have you known others besides Odile in his life?'

'Oh no – but I feel it. You see he is a man who is rather repelled by devotion and passionate love . . . However I say that without really knowing anything about it; I know him so little, it is only what I imagine. At the time I used to meet him I saw something futile and frivolous in his character which rather lowered him in my eyes. But you know, whatever I say is of no importance – I have never seen much of him.'

I felt very uneasy; this seemed to please her. Was Philippe right? Was she really malicious? When I got home I spent a wretched evening. I had found an affectionate letter from Philippe awaiting me and I wanted to ask his pardon for doubting him. Certainly he was weak, but I loved this weakness and interpreted Misa's ambiguous remarks about him as the result of her disappointed love. She asked me several times to go out with her again and invited me to dinner, but I refused.

XVIII

When the time approached for Philippe's return I was indescribably happy. My health was restored and the thought of the life that was forming itself within me made me calm and serene. I did my utmost to give Philippe a pleasant impression when he came home. He must have seen beautiful women and lovely houses in America. In spite of my condition, or because of it, I took extra trouble with my clothes and rearranged the furniture in accordance with hints I had picked up from Misa about Odile's taste. The day Philippe arrived I filled the house with a profusion of white flowers. For once I overcame what he called my 'sordid economy'.

As he stepped out of the train at the Gare Saint-Lazare he looked rejuvenated, happy and sunburnt from six days at sea. He had a great deal to tell me and to talk about.

The first days were very pleasant. Solange was still in Morocco – a fact I had already made sure of. Before resuming his work Philippe took a week's holiday which he devoted entirely to me.

One morning I went out early for a fitting, leaving Philippe in bed. When I returned he told me that a man whose voice he did not know had telephoned and asked for 'Mme Marcenat'; he replied that he was M Marcenat, and the person rang off at once. He telephoned to the supervisor to ask who had rung and was told:

'A call box from the Bourse,' which explained nothing.

'Who could have rung you up from the Bourse?' he asked me.

'From the Bourse?'

'Yes. Someone asked for you and rang off as soon as I gave my name.'

'What an extraordinary thing – are you sure?'

'That question is unworthy of you Isabelle. I am quite sure, the voice was perfectly clear.'

'A man's or a woman's voice?'

'A man's of course.'

'Why of course?'

We had never spoken to each other like that before; I could not help showing embarrassment. Although he had said it was a man's voice I felt sure it was Misa who often rang me up but I dared not mention her name. I was annoyed with Philippe who seemed resentful and suspicious. Could he be jealous? Dear Philippe! If he had realised to what extent I existed only through and for him he would soon have been reassured – even too much so. After lunch he said, in a casual way that reminded me of some of my own questions:

'What are you doing this afternoon?'

'Nothing special – shopping – then I'm going to tea with Mme Brémont at five o'clock.'

'Would you mind my coming with you as I have nothing special to do today?'

'On the contrary, I should be delighted. I am not accustomed to so much attention! I will meet you there at six.'

'What? You told me five.'

'Well, you know how it is at tea parties, the card says five but no one arrives before six.'

'Couldn't I come shopping with you?'

'Certainly . . . I thought you wanted to go to the office to open your mail?'

'There's no hurry. I'll go tomorrow.'

'How nice you are when you have just returned from a journey, Philippe.'

So he came out with me and I felt that there was an atmosphere of constraint between us which was quite new. There is an entry in his notebook about this occasion which revealed feelings towards me that I had never imagined possible.

It seems to me that during my absence she has acquired a certain strength and self-confidence that she had never shown before. Why? It is curious. As she got out of the car to buy some books she gave me an affectionate but strange look. At Mme Brémont's she had a long talk with Dr Gaulin. I found myself trying to hear the tone of their conversation. Gaulin was telling her of biological experiments he had made in his laboratory.

'How interesting!' said Isabelle. 'I should like to see them.'

'Come to my laboratory and I will show you.'

Then for a moment it seemed to me that it was Gaulin's voice I had heard on the telephone.

I had never understood before how absurd jealousy can be, for no suspicion could have been more unfounded. Dr Gaulin was a friendly, intelligent man who had become the fashion that year in society and I enjoyed hearing him talk, but I could not have conceived being attracted by him. Since my marriage to Philippe I had been incapable of even seeing any other man; and yet on a piece of paper pinned by Philippe to the above note I read this:

Accustomed as I am to confuse love with the suffering of doubt and suspicion, I begin to think that I am once again being subjected to this painful experience. The same Isabelle who three months ago I thought too attentive, too constantly present, I now try to keep near me as much as I can. Did I really have that feeling of hopeless boredom in her company? Now I seem less happy but I am not bored for a moment. She is very surprised at my new attitude; she is too modest to grasp the real meaning of it. This morning she said:

'If you don't mind I shall go this afternoon to the Pasteur Institute to see Gaulin's experiments.'

'Certainly not,' I said, 'you will not go.'

She looked stupefied by my vehemence.

'But why Philippe? You heard what he was talking about the other day; it seems to me very interesting.'

'Gaulin has a way of behaving with women that I dislike.'

'Gaulin? What a strange idea! I have met him often this winter and never noticed anything of the kind. But you hardly know him, you only saw him for ten minutes at the Brémont's . . .'

'Exactly, it was during those ten minutes . . .'

And then for the first time since I have known her, Isabelle smiled in a way that recalled Odile.

I remember that scene vividly. I was amused and rather gratified. Suddenly a side of Philippe's nature was disclosed to me that I had hitherto been unaware of. I knew from reading the story of his past life how he had been tortured and held by his jealousy of Odile, but I did not know that I also had the power to use this weapon to bind him closer to me.

It was a temptation but I had no wish to play such a part and was incapable of sustained pretence or hypocrisy. I feel that love should be something greater than a cruel war between lovers.

In a few days I succeeded in restoring Philippe's peace of

mind, shut myself up almost completely and did not see Gaulin again. The last months before my child was born were trying. I felt that my appearance was unsightly and did not want to go about with Philippe for fear of embarrassing him. He gave me all his time during the last weeks and often read aloud to me. Never before had our marriage been nearer to what I had always dreamed of. We re-read several great novels. In my youth I read Balzac and Tolstoy but had not quite understood them. Everything now appeared to have a richer meaning. Dolly in the opening of *Anna Karenina* was like me. Anna herself had a little of Odile and a little of Solange; As Philippe read it I was sure he was making the same comparisons as I was. Sometimes a passage reminded him so strongly of certain aspects of our life that he raised his eyes from the book and we exchanged a smile of understanding. I should have been very happy if Philippe had not still seemed sad. He made no complaint, was in good health, but often sighed; he sat in an armchair by my bed, stretching out his long arms wearily and passing his hands over his eyes.

'Are you tired, darling?' I asked him.

'Yes, a little, I think I need a change of air. That office all day long . . .'

'Of course – specially as you then stay with me all the evening. But do go out, darling . . . enjoy yourself. Why do you no longer go to a theatre or a concert?'

'You know quite well, I hate going alone.'

'Won't Solange be coming back soon? She was only going to be away for two months. Have you any news of her?'

'Yes, she wrote to me. She prolonged her visit, she did not want to leave her husband alone.'

'What? Why, she leaves him every year. Why this sudden solicitude?'

'How should I know?' said Philippe angrily. 'That's what she writes to me and it's all I can tell you.'

XIX

At last Solange returned, a few weeks before my confinement; it was heartrending to see Philippe's sudden transformation. One evening I found him young and gay again. He brought me flowers and some large pink prawns that I liked. He walked round and round my bed, his hands in his pockets, was very lively and told me amusing stories about his office and publishers he had seen during the day. I wondered what was the cause of his sudden high spirits.

He dined at my bedside and casually, without looking at him, I asked:

'Still no news from Solange?'

'What?' he said, with exaggerated casualness, 'didn't I tell you? She rang up this morning – she has been in Paris since yesterday.'

'I am glad for your sake, Philippe. You will have someone to go out with when I am unable to keep you company.'

'But you are absurd, Isabelle, I shall not leave you for a moment.'

'I insist on your going out, anyhow I shall not be alone, my mother will soon be in Paris.'

'That's true,' he said, looking delighted, 'she can't be far away now. Where did her last telegram come from?'

'It was a radio message from the boat, but from what I was told at the shipping office she should be at Suez tomorrow.'

'I am very pleased on your account; it is good of her to take such a long journey to be present at a confinement.'

'My family is like yours, Philippe; births and deaths are festivals. I remember that the funerals of provincial cousins were amongst my father's pleasantest memories.'

'When my Marcenat grandfather was very old he complained bitterly that his doctor forbade him to go to a burial service. "They don't want me to follow poor Ludovic's funeral procession," he said, "though I have so few distractions."'

'You seem in good form this evening, Philippe.'

'Not particularly . . . but it is lovely weather, you are well and this nine months' nightmare is nearly over – naturally I am thankful.'

I was humiliated to see him so lively and to know the cause of his renewed vitality. That evening he ate as he did at St Moritz, with the good appetite which, to my great concern, he had lost for many months. After dinner he became restless and began to yawn. I said:

'Shall we read a little? That Stendhal you began last night was very good . . .'

'Oh yes – *Lamiel* – it isn't bad . . . if you like.'

He assumed a bored expression.

'Listen, Philippe, do you know what you ought to do? Go and say good evening to Solange; you have not seen her for five months.'

'I don't want to leave you. And I have no idea if she is at home, or free. The first evening of her return she must have her family there, or Jacques'.'

'Ring her up.'

I had hoped he would show more resistance but he gave way to the temptation at once.

'All right – I'll try,' he said, and left the room.

Five minutes later he came back looking radiant.

'As you don't mind I'll just run over to Solange's. I shall only stay a quarter of an hour.'

'Stay as long as you like. I am delighted, it will do you good. But come and say goodnight to me when you get back, even if it is very late.'

'It won't be. It is nine o'clock – I shall be home at a quarter to ten.'

I saw him again at midnight. While I waited I read a little and cried a great deal.

XX

My mother arrived from China a few days before the birth of my child. Seeing her again I was astonished to feel nearer to her in a certain way and yet further removed from her than I expected to be. She criticised our way of living, our servants, furniture and friends. Her opinions struck invisible and remote chords that produced faint echoes in me. But our old family traditions were already undermined by Philippe's influence and things which surprised and shocked her, seemed quite natural to me.

She was quick to notice that Philippe was not as attentive to me in those last days of waiting as he might have been.

'I shall keep you company this evening as I don't suppose your husband will have the courage to stay at home.'

I was ashamed that I suffered more from my pride than from my love. I regretted that my mother had not been there before Solange's return, when Philippe never left me except for the hours he was at work. I should like to have shown her that I too could be loved. Often, standing at the foot of my bed, she looked at me in a critical way which revived all the agonies of my girlhood. Watchful, almost hostile, she put her finger on the parting of my hair, saying: 'You are going grey.' It was true.

When Philippe returned home after midnight and passers-by in the street became less frequent, I listened to their footsteps hoping to recognise his. I can still hear that deceptive sound which grows louder and awakens hope as it pauses, then continues, grows fainter and fades away. A man who is going to stop, begins to reduce his pace when a few yards away from his door; at last I heard Philippe's step and noticed his diminishing speed; the light sound of a bell rang through the house, a distant door slammed – it was he. I had made up my mind to be cheerful and indulgent but each time received him with complaints. The monotony and violence of my own words shocked me.

'Oh!' said Philippe wearily. 'I can't stand any more, Isabelle, I assure you . . . Can't you see how incoherent you are? . . . It is you who implore me to go out, I do as you ask and then you load me with reproaches. What is it you want? That I should shut myself up in this house? I will do it. Yes – I promise I will . . . anything rather than these incessant quarrels . . . But I beg you not to be generous at nine o'clock in the evening and just the opposite at midnight . . .'

'Yes, Philippe, it's true . . . I am hateful. I swear I won't do it again.'

But the next time some demon within me dictated the same useless remarks. My anger was chiefly directed against Solange. I thought that at such a moment she might let me have my husband.

She came to see me. Conversation was rather difficult. She wore a beautiful sable coat and recommended her furrier to me at length. Then Philippe arrived; she must have told him she was coming because he returned earlier than usual. The coat became a useless, almost invisible accessory and the garden at Marrakesh took its place.

'You can't imagine what it is like, Isabelle . . . In the morning I walk with bare feet on the warm tiles, amongst orange trees . . . roses and jasmine entwine every column. One sees pale blue humming-birds through the flowers and leaves . . . and far beyond the roofs the snow on the Atlas mountains, glitters like fine diamonds . . . ('we have already had the diamonds at St. Moritz', I thought) . . . And the nights! The moon that the cypress tree seems to be pointing at with a black finger . . . An Arab playing a guitar in the neighbouring garden . . . Oh Marcenat, Marcenat, how I love it!'

With her head thrown back she seemed to be breathing in the scent of jasmin and roses. When she left Philippe took her to the door. He returned looking slightly embarrassed and stood with his back against the fireplace in my room. After a long silence he said:

'You ought to come with me to Morocco some time . . . it is really very beautiful . . . By the way, I've brought you a book by Robert Etienne about the Berbers – their private lives . . . It is a kind of novel . . . and also a poem. It's amazing.'

'Poor Philippe, how I pity you, having to deal with women. What hypocrites they are!'

'What makes you say that, Isabelle?'

'I say it because it is true; I know women well and they are so uninteresting.'

At last I felt the first pains; the confinement was long and difficult. Philippe's emotion gratified me, he was white and more frightened than I was. I saw how much my life meant to him. His fear gave me courage and trying to reassure him helped me to control my own nervousness. I talked of our little boy, feeling certain of having a son.

'We will call him Alain, Philippe. He will have eyebrows rather too high up like yours – and will walk up and down with his hands in his pockets when he is worried . . . he is sure to be worried, poor Alain, isn't he, Philippe? The son of such parents . . . What a heredity!'

Philippe tried to smile, but I could see that he was deeply moved. When I felt worse I asked him to hold my hand.

'Do you remember my hand on yours at *Siegfried*? . . . that was the beginning of everything.'

A little later I heard from my room Dr Crès saying to Philippe:

'Your wife is astonishingly brave; I have seldom seen such courage.'

'Yes – my wife is a very fine person. I only hope nothing will happen to her.'

'What could happen? Everything is normal.'

They gave me chloroform towards the end; it was not my wish. When I opened my eyes I saw Philippe standing beside me looking tender and happy. He kissed my hand:

'We have a son, darling.'

I wanted to see him but was disappointed.

My mother and Philippe's were installed in the little sitting-room next to my bedroom. The door was open, and with closed eyes, half asleep, I heard their depressing forebodings about the education of the child. Although they were very different and no doubt disagreed on nearly all subjects, they discovered a mutual loyalty to their own generation by finding fault with the young couple.

'Of course,' said my mother, 'these young people think only of happiness. Children must be happy, the husband must be happy, the mistress of the house must be happy and so must the servants, and to achieve this they abolish rules, do away with restrictions, will have no punishments or prohibitions and everything is pardoned, not only before pardon is deserved but even before it is asked. It is incomprehensible. My daughter, for instance, tells me she is not happy. It is not Philippe's fault, he is a very good husband and does not run after women more than most men. No, it is because she analyses herself, is always anxiously examining the barometer of their "love", as she puts it . . . Have you ever troubled much about the temperature of your marriage? I haven't. I tried to help my husband in his career; I had a difficult house to run, we were very busy and everything went well . . . It is the same with the education of children. Isabelle says that above all she wants Alain to have a happier childhood than she had. I can assure you hers was not unpleasant. I brought her up rather severely, I don't regret it – you see the result.'

'If you had not brought her up as you did,' said Mme Marcenat, also talking very softly, 'Isabelle would never have become the delightful woman she is. She should be very grateful to you and so should my son.'

I kept quite still because the conversation amused me. Who knows, I thought! Perhaps they are right.

Since the much longed for birth of our child everything disappointed me. I had formed such great hopes that the reality could not satisfy them. I believed that the child would be a new and powerful link between Philippe and me. It was not so. He took very little interest in his son, went to see him once a day, amused himself by talking English with the nurse for a few minutes and then became once more the

Philippe I had always known, aloof and kind but with a vague mist of longing that pervaded his melancholy amiability. He seemed now to be suffering from something more than boredom. Philippe was unhappy. He did not go out so often which I first thought was out of consideration for me, and that he had scruples about leaving me alone while I was still weak. Several times when my mother or a friend were coming to see me I said:

'Philippe I know these family conversations bore you – ring up Solange and take her to the cinema this evening.'

'Why do you always want to force me to go out with Solange? I can live for two days without seeing her.'

Poor Philippe! That's just what he could not do. Without knowing exactly why, or anything about Solange's private life I felt there was something changed in their relationship since she had returned from Morocco, and that Philippe was suffering on her account. I dared not question him, but just from the look on his face I could follow the course of his moral sickness. In a few weeks he had grown unbelievably thinner; his complexion was yellow, and his eyes looked weary. He complained of sleeping badly and had the fixed expression of a person suffering from insomnia. At meals he was silent, then made an effort to talk, which was even more painful to me than his silence.

Renée came to see me and brought a little dress for Alain. I saw at once that she was transformed. She had organised her life of work and talked of Dr Gaulin in a way that made me think he was her lover. For some months this liaison had been referred to at Gandumas, but only as a false rumour. The family wanted to keep on cordial terms with Renée and were afraid that their own code would forbid them to receive her if they admitted her virtue to be in doubt. But when I saw her I knew that the Marcenats, consciously or not, were wrong. Renée had the joyful air of a woman who loves and is loved.

Since my marriage I had been estranged from Renée and the few times we had met I found her hard and almost hostile. But this time we resumed at once the same friendly tone of our long wartime conversations. We began to talk of Philippe – and to talk of him intimately. For the first time Renée told me with great frankness that she had loved him and our marriage had made her very unhappy.

'At that moment I almost hated you,' she said, 'then I began to arrange my life differently, and now that distressing period seems unreal to me. Our strongest emotions die, don't you think so? I look back upon myself as I was three years ago with the same curiosity and indifference as if I were looking at another woman.'

'Perhaps I have not yet got to that stage, Renée, I still love Philippe as much as I did at the beginning – even more and feel capable of making sacrifices for him now that I would not have made six months ago.'

Renée looked at me for a moment without speaking, like a doctor.

'I believe you,' she said at last, 'I told you just now, Isabelle, that I regret nothing; I feel more strongly than that about it. Forgive my being frank. I congratulate myself every day that I am not married to Philippe.'

'And I congratulate myself that I am.'

'Yes, I know, because you love him and you have adopted his habit of seeking happiness in suffering. But Philippe is a terrible person; there is nothing bad in him – quite the contrary – but terrible because he is obsessed. I knew him as a child. He was just the same, except perhaps at that time there were other possibilities in him. Then Odile came and fixed once for all his personality as a lover. For him love is closely associated with a certain type of face, a certain recklessness of action, a certain disquieting grace that is not entirely honest. And as at the same time he is terribly sensitive, this type of woman, the only kind he can love, makes him very unhappy. Isn't that true?'

'It is true and not true, Renée. I know it always sounds absurd to say "I am loved", yet Philippe does love me, I cannot doubt it . . . only at the same time he also needs quite a different kind of woman – like Odile, or Solange . . . Do you know Solange Villier?'

'Very well . . . I did not like to speak of her, but it was she I was thinking of.'

'Yes – you can speak of her. I am no longer jealous; I have been . . . Do people say that Solange is Philippe's mistress?'

'Oh no . . . in fact they are saying that during her last visit to Morocco she fell in love with Robert Etienne – you know, the man who wrote such an interesting book about the Berbers . . . Latterly she spent all her time with him in Marrakesh. He has just returned to Paris . . . He is a great writer and a charming man; Gaulin thinks very highly of him.'

I reflected for a moment. Yes – it was just what I had imagined and the name Etienne explained some of Philippe's conversations. He had brought home, one after the other, all Etienne's books and read extracts aloud, asking me what I thought. I liked them, specially the long meditation entitled 'Prayer in the Garden of the Oudaïas'.

'It is beautiful,' Philippe had said, 'Yes – it is really beautiful – and primitive.'

My poor Philippe! How he must have suffered. No doubt he now analysed Solange's every word and gesture, as he had long ago analysed Odile's, to seek traces in them of the unknown man; probably it was in this vain and torturing research that he passed his sleepless nights. How furious I suddenly felt with that woman!

'It is so true, Renée, what you said just now about the habit of seeking pleasure in suffering . . . But when through circumstances one's emotional life begins like that as with Philippe and me, is it still possible to change oneself?'

'I believe it is always possible if one wishes it strongly enough.'

'But how could the desire to do so arise unless the change had already taken place?'

'Gaulin would answer: "By understanding the mechanism and mastering it" . . . that's to say, by being more intelligent.'

'But Philippe is intelligent.'

'Very, but he gives way too much to his sensibility and does not use his intelligence enough.'

We argued happily till Philippe came home. Renée had a scientific way of discussing things, which I liked as it made me feel that I resembled many others and was just in a class labelled 'Les Amoureuses'.

Philippe seemed pleased to find Renée, asked her to stay to dinner and for the first time for several weeks talked with animation throughout the meal. He was interested in science and she told him of new experiments. As she mentioned Gaulin's name for the second time he said to her abruptly: 'Do you know Gaulin well?'

'Indeed I do, he is my chief.'

'Isn't he a friend of Robert Etienne, the one from Morocco, who wrote "The Prayer to the Oudaïas"?'

'Yes.'

'And do you know Etienne?'

'Very well.'

'What kind of man is he?'

'Remarkable.'

'Oh,' said Philippe, and added with difficulty, 'yes, I also think he has talent . . . but sometimes it happens that a man is inferior to his work . . .'

'It is not so in his case,' said Renée, pitilessly.

I looked at her beseechingly. Philippe was silent for the rest of the evening.

XXI

Philippe's love for Solange Villier was ebbing away before my eyes. He never spoke of it and evidently wanted me to think that nothing was changed between them. He still saw her often, but not nearly so often as before. Their meetings no longer gave him unmixed pleasure. When they had been out together he did not return young and happy but at times almost in despair. There were moments when he seemed on the point of confiding in me. He took my hand and said:

'Isabelle, it is you who have chosen the better way.'

'Why darling?'

'Because . . .'

Then he stopped, but I understood.

Philippe continued to send flowers to Solange and to treat her as though he loved her. Don Quixote and Lancelot remained faithful. But the notes I found among his papers for the year 1923 are very sad.

April 17th. Walk with Solange . . .Montmarte. We went up as far as the Place du Tertre and sat on the terrace of a café. Croissants and lemonade. She asked for a bar of chocolate and enjoyed it like a little girl. I experienced exactly the same sensations as in the long forgotten Odile-François days. Solange wants to be natural, is affectionate and shows great kindness. But I can see she is thinking of someone else. She seems to have the same languor as Odile had after her first escape and, like her, eludes all explanations. When I want to talk about ourselves she is evasive and invents some game. Today she amused herself by imagining the lives of the passers-by from their appearance and gestures. She made up quite a story about a taxi driver who arrived in front of our café with two women. I try not to love her any more but do not succeed. She is as seductive as ever – her air of radiant health – her sunburnt complexion . . .

'My dear,' she said, 'you are sad. What is the matter? Don't you find life amusing? Just think, in each of those funny little houses there are men and women whose lives would be interesting to observe. There are hundreds of places like this in Paris and dozens of places like Paris in the world. It is really marvellous!'

'I don't agree with you, Solange; I think life is an interesting spectacle when one is very young, but by the time one reaches the age of forty, as I have, and discovers the prompter, the actors' devices and the cunning tricks of those who pull the strings, it is time to leave.'

'You must not talk like that. You have seen nothing yet.'

'Indeed I have, my poor Solange. I've seen the third act; I don't find it very good or very amusing; it is always the same situation, and always will be. I've had enough and do not wish to wait for the end.'

'You are a bad audience – you have a delightful wife and charming women friends . . .'

'Women friends?'

'Yes you have, I know your life.'

All this is terribly 'Odile'. I cannot forgive myself for my weak acceptance and my melancholy defeat. I ought to give up seeing Solange and then perhaps I might be at peace. To see her and not love her is impossible.

April 18th. Last night I had a long conversation about love with one of my friends who is supposed to have been a great Don Juan of his time. He is over fifty and I was struck by how little happiness these love affairs, for which he was much envied, had given him.

'Really,' he said, 'I have only loved one woman – Claire P . . ., and how weary I became even of her towards the end!'

'And yet – she is charming!'

'Oh you can't judge her now. She is affected and exaggerates the mannerisms that were formerly natural to her. No, I can't even look at her any more.'

'And the others?'

'They meant nothing to me.'

Then I mentioned the woman who is said to fill his life at present.

He said, 'I don't care for her at all. We meet from force of habit. She has made me suffer horribly and has been very unfaithful. Now I see her as she is. She is really nothing to me.'

He made me wonder if romantic love exists and whether one should give up the whole idea. Only death saves it from disintegration. (*Tristan.*)

April 19th. Visit to Gandumas. The first for three months. Some workmen came to tell me of their difficulties – poverty, sickness. At the sight of these real troubles I blushed for my imaginary ones. And yet, amongst these men also, there are emotional dramas. Passed a whole night without sleep, meditating on my life. I think it has been one long mistake. From the outside I appear to have had a career. In reality my object in life has been to find absolute happiness through women and there is no more hopeless quest. Perfect love does not exist, any more than a perfect government. Above all one must avoid deceiving oneself. Our feelings are too often misleading. I could rid myself of the obsession of Solange in an instant if I consented to look at her true picture, which has been in my mind ever since I knew her, drawn by an accurate and cruel master, though I refuse to see it.

April 20th. Although Solange no longer cares for me, when I try to free myself she slightly tightens the cord. Coquetry or charity?

April 23rd. Where did I go wrong? Solange has evolved like Odile. Is this because I have made the same mistakes? Or because I made a similar choice? Is it always necessary to hide one's feelings and use diplomacy to keep a woman's love? I don't know.

April 27th. Every ten years one should discard ideas that have proved false and dangerous.

Ideas to be discarded:

(*a*) *That women can be bound by a promise or a vow.* Women have no morals. Their behaviour depends on those they love.

(*b*) *That there exists a perfect woman with whom love would be a series of unmixed joys of the senses, the mind and the heart.* Two human beings moored close together are like two vessels rocked by the waves; their hulls run foul of each other and creak.

May 28th. Dinner at Avenue Marceau. Aunt Cora expiring amongst her capons and orchids. Hélène came to talk to me about Solange.

'Poor Marcenat! How miserable you have been looking for several weeks . . . I understand. Naturally you are unhappy.'

'I don't know what you are talking about,' I replied.

'Yes, you do,' she said, 'you still love her.'

I protested.

XXII

The red notebook shows me now a Philippe much more lucid and more in command of himself than he appeared to me when he wrote these notes in 1923. I think his intelligence was already freer but Philippe the slave was still hidden in the secret depths of his being. He looked so miserable that several times I considered going to see Solange and telling her of my anxiety about him, but such a step seemed so mad that I dared not take it. Anyhow I now hated Solange and felt that once alone with her I might not be able to control myself. We continued to meet her at the Thianges, then Philippe refused to go to Hélène's parties, which he had never done before.

'You go,' he said, 'to show we are not offended with her. That would be unfair, Hélène is so kind, but I cannot go there again. The older I get the more I dislike society . . . My own fireside, a book, you . . . that is my happiness now.'

I knew he was sincere but I also knew that if at this moment he had met an attractive and frivolous young woman who, by an imperceptible glance had given him the signal he was waiting for, he would immediately have changed his philosophy and explained that after a day's work he needed above all to see new people and amuse himself. When I was first married I used to be saddened by the knowledge that the thoughts of those we love are forever concealed from us. But Philippe had now become transparent to me. I could perceive all his thoughts, all his weaknesses, but I loved him more than ever. One evening in his study I remember looking at him for a long time without speaking.

'What are you thinking about?' he asked, smiling.

'I am trying to see you as if I did not love you, and love you all the same.'

'Good heavens! How complicated. And can you do it?'

'Love you as you are? Yes, easily.'

That evening he suggested our going to Gandumas earlier than usual.

'There is nothing to keep us in Paris. I can look after my

business just as well from there. The country air will be excellent for Alain and my mother will not be so lonely. It would be an advantage in every way.'

This arrangement was all I could desire. At Gandumas Philippe would belong to me. My only fear was that he might be bored but soon after our arrival his spirits began to revive. While we were in Paris, although he had lost Solange, he clung tenaciously to a hope, no doubt a vain one. He made an instinctive gesture when he heard the telephone ring, which proved he was not yet cured. When we were out together I was painfully aware of his every reaction and knew that though he dreaded meeting Solange he hoped to do so. He still cared terribly for her and she could have got him back at once if she had wanted to. Gandumas and its surroundings had no associations with Solange and Philippe gradually began to forget her. By the end of a week he already looked better; his cheeks were fuller, his eyes brighter and he slept well.

The weather was fine and we went for long walks. Philippe told me he wanted in future to follow his father's example and take more interest in his estate. We went to the three farms, Guichardie, Bruyères and Resonzac. He spent the mornings at the factory and every afternoon we went out together.

'Do you know what we ought to do?' he said. 'Take a book and read aloud in the forest.'

There were beautiful shady spots around Gandumas; we would sit on the moss at the edge of a path over which branches intermingled, forming soft green arches; sometimes on a fallen tree-trunk or on one of the seats placed there long ago by his grandfather. Philippe would read aloud parts of his favourite books. Occasionally he looked up and said:

'Am I boring you?'

'What an idea! I have never been so happy in my life.'

After he had finished we discussed the characters in the book and often went on to talk about real people. One day I brought a little book whose title I refused to show him.

'What is this mysterious book?' he said.

'It is one I have taken from your mother's library and which played a part in your life, at least so you wrote me before we were married.'

'I know, it's my *Petits Soldats Russes*. Oh, I'm so glad you found it, Isabelle. Give it to me.'

He turned over the pages and seemed amused and a little disappointed: '"*They proposed electing a queen; she was a remarkably beautiful, slender, elegant and skilful girl . . . bowing our heads before her we vowed to obey the laws.*"'

'Oh, it is charming, Philippe, and so like you . . . There is also a nice story: an object desired by the queen which the hero goes to seek with great difficulty . . . Wait . . . Pass me the book . . .'

'"*Good heavens!' said the queen, 'how much trouble you have taken! Thank you!' She was very pleased. In shaking my hand again when I was saying goodbye to her she added: 'If I am still your queen, I shall tell the General to give you a special reward.' I bowed to her and withdrew; I was very happy.*"'

'You have remained that little boy all your life, Philippe . . . only the queen has often changed.'

Philippe, seated under a bush, was breaking off little twigs that he snapped between his fingers and threw on the grass.

'Yes,' he said, 'the queen has often changed. The truth is I have never yet met the queen . . . at least not the perfect one.'

'Who was the queen, Philippe?'

'Several women, my darling. Denise Aubry, a little . . .

but a very imperfect one. Did I tell you she is dead, poor Denise Aubry?'

'No, Philippe . . . She must have been quite young? . . . What did she die of?'

'I don't know; my mother told me the other day. It had a strange effect on me to hear as an unimportant item of news that a woman who was for several years the centre of my world had died.'

'After Denise Aubry, who was the queen?'

'Odile.'

'It was she who was the nearest to the queen of your dreams?'

'Yes, because she was so beautiful.'

'And after Odile? . . . Hélène de Thianges a little?'

'A little, perhaps, but certainly you Isabelle.'

'I too? Is that true? For how long?'

'A very long time.'

'Then Solange?'

'Yes, then Solange . . .'

'Is Solange still the queen, Philippe?'

'No, but in spite of everything, my memories of her mean a great deal to me. She was so alive, so strong. I felt younger and happier when I was with her.'

'You must see her again, Philippe.'

'Yes, I will when I am really cured, but she will no longer be the queen; that is finished.'

'And now, Philippe, who is the queen?'

He hesitated a moment, then looking at me said:

'You are.'

'But I was deposed long ago.'

'Yes, perhaps, because you were jealous, petty and unjust. But you have been so brave for the last three months, so kind and straightforward, that I have given you back your crown. You can't imagine how you have changed, Isabelle. You are no longer the same woman.'

'I know that is true, dearest. A woman really in love has no personality; she says she has and wants to believe it, but it is not true. No, she tries to understand what sort of woman her lover hopes to find in her – and become that woman . . . With you, Philippe, it is very difficult because one doesn't quite know what you want. You need fidelity and tenderness, but you also need coquetry and uncertainty. What can one do? I have chosen the part of fidelity, which is nearest to my nature . . . But I believe for a long time you will also need someone unstable and more elusive. The great victory I have won over myself is that I accept the other one with resignation even with satisfaction. What I have learnt during the last year is very valuable. I have discovered that if one really loves, one must not attach too much importance to the actions of the beloved. We need him; only he can enable us to live in a certain "atmosphere" which we cannot do without. Hélène quite rightly calls it "climate". So long as we can keep and preserve him, good heavens, what does anything else matter? Life is so short, so difficult . . . should I have the right, my poor Philippe, to deprive you if I could of a few hours' happiness that you can get from these women? Yes, I have improved, I am no longer jealous; I don't suffer any more.'

Philippe stretched himself out on the grass and rested his head on my lap.

'I have not reached that point yet,' he said, 'I think I could still suffer a great deal. The shortness of life is no consolation to me. It is short, that's true, but in relation to what? For us it is everything . . . All the same I feel that I am slowly entering a more tranquil zone. Do you remember, Isabelle, when I likened my life to a symphony in which different themes mingle, the theme of the Knight, that of the Cynic and that of the Rival? I still hear them all very clearly. But I can also hear in the orchestra a single instrument, I don't know which it is, that repeats with quiet insistence a theme consisting of a few tender and satisfying bars. It is the theme of serenity and resembles that of old age.'

'But you are young, Philippe.'

'Yes, that is why the theme seems very faint. Later it will permeate the whole orchestra and then I shall regret that the time has passed for me to hear the others.'

'What saddens me sometimes, Philippe, is that the apprenticeship is so long. You tell me I have improved and I believe it is true. At forty perhaps I shall begin to understand life a little, but it will be too late . . . Do you believe it is possible, darling, that two beings can be perfectly united, without a shadow?'

'It has been possible during the last hour,' said Philippe as he got up.

XXIII

The happiest period of my married life was that summer at Gandumas. I think Philippe loved me twice; for a few weeks before our marriage and during these last three months from June to September when I felt he loved me without reserve. His mother had insisted on our sharing a room; she attached great importance to it and could not understand how a husband and wife could occupy separate rooms. This made us still more united. Alain came to play with us in the mornings;

his teeth were troubling him but he did not make a fuss. When he cried Philippe said:

'You must smile, Alain!' And I believe the child understood what he meant, because he made an effort to stop crying, and to look happy. Philippe began to love his son.

The weather was wonderful. When Philippe returned from the factory he liked to bask in the sun; two armchairs were put on the lawn in front of the house and we sat there silent and lost in vague dreams. I liked to think that the same images filled our minds: the heath, the ruined château of Chardeuil shimmering in the hot air, further off the shrouded curves of the hills, beyond that perhaps Solange's face and the rather hard look in her beautiful eyes; on the horizon, no doubt, a Florentine landscape with wide, gently sloping roofs and domes and cypresses replacing the fir trees on the hills, then the angelic face of Odile . . . Yes, in my mind too there were pictures of Odile and Solange; it was inevitable. Sometimes Philippe looked at me and smiled. I knew we were truly united and I was happy. The dinner bell summoned us from this luxurious langour.

'Oh Philippe, I should love to spend my whole life like this, beside you, bemused, holding your hand in the warm air . . . It is lovely and yet so melancholy. I wonder why?'

'Very beautiful moments are always melancholy. We feel they are fleeting. We want to hold on to them, but cannot. When I was a child I always felt like that at a circus, later on at a concert when I was too happy. I thought to myself: "In two hours it will be all over."'

'But now, Philippe, we have thirty years before us.'

'It is a very short time, thirty years.'

'Oh I don't ask for more.'

'My mother-in-law seemed to respond to our happiness.

'At last,' she said one evening, 'I see Philippe living as I always wished him to. Do you know what you should do if you are wise? Make Philippe return completely to Gandumas. Paris is no good to him. He is like his father who was really shy and sensitive in spite of his air of independence. All the excitement of Paris, all the complex emotions, make Philippe ill.'

'I am afraid he would get tired of being here.'

'I don't think so. His father and I lived here for sixteen years – the best time of our lives.'

'Yes, but Philippe has acquired different habits. I know I should be happier because I like living alone with him, but he . . .'

'He would have you.'

'I don't think that would always be enough for him.'

'You are too modest, dear Isabelle, and have no confidence in yourself. You mustn't give up the struggle like that.'

'I am not giving up the struggle . . . far from it, I am now certain I shall win . . . I shall outlast the others, whereas they will be forgotten and will hardly count in his life . . .'

'The others!' said my mother-in-law, surprised, 'you really are strangely weak.'

She was gentle but tenacious and often returned to her idea, but I was careful not to speak of it to Philippe. I knew that such a suggestion would at once destroy the perfect harmony we were enjoying. In fact my fear that he might be bored made me propose several times spending Sundays with neighbours or going with him to see parts of Perigord or Limousin he had mentioned and which I knew very little. I liked him to show me his own countryside and loved this rather wild province with its great thick-walled châteaux set on mountain peaks whence one could discern soft landscapes and rivers about which Philippe told me legends and stories. I, who had so loved French history, was moved to hear again the names: Hautefort, Biron, Brantome. Occasionally I shyly connected Philippe's story with something I had read and was pleased when he listened to me attentively.

'What a lot of things you know, Isabelle,' he said, 'you are very intelligent, perhaps more than any other woman.'

'Please don't laugh at me, Philippe.'

I felt as though I had been discovered at last by a man whom I had loved a long time without hope.

XXIV

Philippe wanted to show me the grottos of the Vezere valley. I liked the dark river winding amongst rocks hollowed out and polished by the water, but the grottos disappointed me. We had to climb steep paths in the oppressive heat, then enter narrow stone passages to look at vague bisons sketched in red on the walls.

'Can you see anything?' I asked Philippe, 'it might be a bison or anything else . . . on the other side.'

'I can see nothing at all – I want to go out, I'm frozen.'

After the heat of the climb I too had a feeling of icy coldness in the cave. Philippe was very quiet on the way home; in the evening he complained of a cold. The next morning he woke me up early.

'I don't feel well,' he said.

I got up in a hurry, drew back the curtains and was alarmed at the sight of his face; he was pale, looked very distressed and his eyes had dark lines round them.

'Yes, you look ill, Philippe, you caught cold yesterday . . .'

'It hurts me to breathe and I am very feverish. It won't be anything, my darling. Give me some aspirin.'

He did not want to see a doctor and I dared not insist, but when I called my mother-in-law at about nine o'clock she took his temperature and treated him with surprising authority as she would a sick child. In spite of his protests she sent for Dr Toury from Chardeuil. He was rather shy and gentle, and looked at you through his horn-rimmed glasses for a long time before speaking. He examined Philippe's chest very carefully with his stethoscope.

'A sharp attack of bronchitis,' he said, 'M Marcenat, you will be laid up for at least a week.'

He made a sign to me to leave the room with him and said, looking somewhat embarrassed:

'Well, Madame Marcenat, it is rather worrying. Your husband has bronchial pneumonia. I can hear a rattle all over his chest, almost the same as in a pulmonary oedema. And then his temperature is 40° and pulse 140 . . . It is acute pneumonia.'

I felt half frozen and did not fully understand.

'But he is not in danger doctor?' I asked, almost jokingly, so unlikely did it seem to me that my vigorous Philippe of the evening before could be very ill. He seemed surprised.

'Pneumonia is always dangerous; one must wait before forming an opinion.' Then he told me what to do.

I remember hardly anything of the days that followed; I had been thrown abruptly into that mythical and cloistered life of illness. I nursed Philippe, doing as much as I could. I felt that useful activity would avert the mysterious and terrible menace. When there was nothing more to do I sat beside him, in a white smock, trying to convey my own strength to him through my eyes. For a long time he continued to recognise me; he was so prostrate that he could not speak, but he thanked me with his eyes. Then he became delirious. There was a dreadful moment for me on the third day because he thought I was Solange. Suddenly in the middle of the night, he began to talk to me with great effort.

'Oh!' he said, 'you have come, my little Solange. I knew you would; it is kind of you.'

He had difficulty in pronouncing the words but looked at me with despairing tenderness.

'My little Solange, kiss me,' he murmured. 'You can, it's all right. I am so ill.'

Without stopping to think I leaned over him and on my lips he kissed Solange. Oh how gladly I would have given you Solange, Philippe, if I had thought her love could save you. I think if I ever loved you perfectly it was at that moment, because I had abdicated; I existed only for you. During that period of delirium my mother-in-law was present several times when Philippe spoke of Solange; not once did I have any feeling of wounded pride. I only said to myself: 'Let him live, oh God, let him live!'

On the fifth day I had a little hope; when I took his temperature in the morning it had gone down, but when the doctor came and I said: 'He is better, only 38°' I saw at once he remained gloomy. He examined Philippe, who was almost unconscious.

'Well,' I said nervously as he got up, 'isn't he better?'

He sighed and looked sadly at me.

'No – on the contrary. I don't like this sudden drop of temperature. It is a bad sign.'

'But not a sign of the end?'

He did not answer.

By the evening Philippe's temperature had risen and his

face was changing in a terrifying way. I knew now that he was going to die; I sat beside him holding his burning hand in mine; he did not seem to feel it. I thought: 'So you are going to leave me, my darling' – and tried to imagine that inconceivable thing – life without Philippe. My God! To think I could have been jealous! . . . he had only a few months to live and . . .

Then I vowed to myself that if, by a miracle Philippe should be saved I would seek no other happiness than his.

At midnight my mother-in-law wanted to relieve me; I shook my head emphatically; but could not speak. I was still holding Philippe's hand. His difficult breathing hurt me. Suddenly he opened his eyes and said:

'Isabelle, I am suffocating; I believe I am going to die.'

These few words were spoken very clearly and then he fell back again in to a coma. His mother took me by the shoulder and kissed me. His pulse, which I held, became imperceptible. At six in the morning the doctor came and gave him an injection which revived him a little. At seven Philippe breathed his last without having regained consciousness. His mother closed his eyes. I thought of a phrase he had written when his father died: 'Shall I have to face death alone some day? I only hope it will be soon.'

It was alas, too soon. If only I could have kept you longer, my beloved, I believe I should have known how to make you happy. But our destinies and our desires are so seldom in tune.